Jerry Perlet's Dragon Stories 4

The Black Fog

By: JERROLD PERLET

Copyright 2015 Jerrold Perlet

To the students of

Monocacy Elementary School

And

Sherwood Elementary School

Where the Dragon began

Author's Notes

Jerry Perlet's Dragon Stories 4: The Black Fog is a continuation of the dragon adventures from **Volume 1: Sara's Adventures** , **Volume 2: George and Zoe's Adventures**, and **Volume 3: The Return of the Red Leprechaun.** The first dragon story was told to a group of students at Monocacy Elementary School in Montgomery County, Maryland as they waited for a late bus. The setting comes from Sugarloaf Mountain and the many farmhouses in the area. The adventures with the dragon were created as a part of the quarterly school assemblies.

As I moved to Sherwood Elementary School, I shared the stories there as well. The children and their parents often asked where they could buy the books that contained the stories. I explained that they came from my imagination and there was no book.   Many families have asked to have the tales written out.

Over the years the students have asked many questions and contributed many ideas to the stories. **The Black Fog** is the fourth volume in the series. I would like to thank the Sherwood Elementary School first graders, Laytonsville Elementary School fifth graders, and The Lucy School students grades 1 to 5, for contributing ideas to the stories in the fourth volume.

I have retired from the Montgomery County Public schools in Maryland after 38 years teaching and as an elementary principal. I have already published **Adventures with Grandpa Ek: Washington DC** and **Adventures with Grandpa Ek: Annapolis,** . Many other stories are in their beginning stages to be released in the future.

I hope you will enjoy the adventures!

Jerry Perlet

grandpaek@yahoo.com

Special Thanks to:

Marie Perlet, my wife and my editor.

Katie and Matthew Perlet for designing the covers.

Thanks to the first grade **students at Sherwood Elementary School**, Maryland, for contributing to Chapters 2, 3, and 9.

Thanks to the fifth grade **students at Laytonsville Elementary School**, Maryland, for contributing to the whole plot of the story and especially Chapters 5, 10, and 12.

Thanks to the primary **students at The Lucy School**, Maryland, for contributing to Chapter 4.

Thanks to the upper grade **students at The Lucy School**, Maryland, for contributing to the whole plot of the story and especially Chapters 5, 10, and 12.

Other children's books by Jerry Perlet:

Adventures with Grandpa Ek: Washington D.C., copyright 1978

Adventures with Grandpa Ek: Annapolis, copyright 2013

Jerry Perlet's Dragon Stories: Sara's Adventures with the Dragon, copyright 2013

Jerry Perlet's Dragon Stories 2: George and Zoe's Adventures with the Dragon, copyright 2013

Jerry Perlet's Dragon Stories 3: The Return of the Red Leprechaun, copyright 2014

Jerry Perlet's Dragon Stories 4: The Black Fog, copyright 2015

Table of Contents

Prologue

Zoe, George, Annie, and Nate stood shoulder to shoulder with their white farmhouse behind them and the mountain behind the house. They faced a swirling black cloud of fog headed right for them. There were flashes of lightning inside the fog. The wind was getting stronger and the noise was deafening.

Zoe yelled, "Are we ready for this?"

The twins responded, "Yeah! Let's do it!"

George yelled above the howling wind, "On my count, we begin Operation Save the Dragon!" The children raised their hands and waited.

"Ready! One....Two....Three...."

* * * * * * * * * * * * * * * * * * *

But wait. What is going on here? How did the children get into this situation? What is that swirling black fog? What has happened?

We must go back a few months to find out.

Chapter 1

<u>Once a Fairy, Always a Fairy</u>

It was a beautiful Saturday morning in late June. The sun was shining brightly, the air was crisp and clean, and the sky was that brilliant blue color of late spring. Zoe sat up in bed. She now had her own bedroom and George had moved into the room across the hallway. The twins were in George and Zoe's old bedroom with the best view of the mountain and the dragon's cave. George's room also looked out across the valley to the mountain. Zoe's room faced the front of the house so she had to visit one of their rooms to see the mountain.

She crept out of bed and tiptoed to George's door. She tapped lightly on the door and then went in. George was out cold, snoring away in Dreamsville. She went to his window and saw the beautiful morning. Zoe took a deep breath and tiptoed to the twins' room, closing George's door behind her. Nate and Annie were already awake sitting in the large window seat staring at the gorgeous morning.

"Zoe! You're awake! Come sit with us!" Annie was always wide awake and ready to go at the crack of dawn. Nate smiled and waved at Zoe to come over and sit with them.

"It's a great day, Zoe. The sun is shining and the sky is so blue and the mountain is glowing with the green colors of the new leaves. It's going to be a wonderful day!"

Zoe joined them in the window seat. Annie and Nate were so lucky to have this view. Zoe knew where the dragon's cave was on the mountain and she pointed to the large boulder near the top. "See the smoke? Looks like the dragon is up and having an early breakfast."

Annie and Nate peered out the window and giggled. "You have the best eyesight, Zoe. I didn't even see that smoke. Why don't you and George ever go with us to the cave anymore? You and the dragon were always so close."

"Well, Nate. Going into middle school has been a really busy time with so much homework and new friends and texting and phoning and things to do. I just haven't found much time to visit the dragon. And George and I can't fit through that little door in the tree anymore either.

"I have climbed up to the boulder and met the dragon there a few times when I really needed to talk to him about something. He is such a good listener and has the best advice. He told me I was growing up and I needed to go it alone. He would always be there in the shadows watching over me, but it is time for me to be on my own. So he will stay here with me." Zoe touched her heart as she gazed at the mountain.

"Good morning, everybody. Mind if I join the party?" George was standing in the doorway listening to Zoe and watching the twins as they gazed at her. She was the best big sister anyone could ever want. The twins waved him over to the window seat. George jumped onto a big cushion on the floor next to them.

Nate asked, "Are you coming with us today, George?"

"Thanks for the offer, but I have a big soccer game today. Our team is in the finals and if we win today, we get trophies. I just graduated from fifth grade and I will be in middle school next year, so I don't think I will have much time for visiting the dragon anymore.

"It really is your time now. You and Annie will go on fantastic adventures with the dragon and he will teach you how to think and solve problems. Be brave, listen, and learn how to be independent. Explore and have fun. I miss those adventures, but I have my own now in school with my friends."

Annie pointed across the room at her bed and waved her finger towards herself. The large blue teddy bear rose up from the bed and floated to her arms. She hugged the bear and said, "But I want you and Zoe to come with us. We love the dragon and you do, too. I could tell when you took us to the cave to meet him. You should come."

George replied, "Annie, we love the dragon, but we can't even fit through the door in the tree anymore. And you need to remember to only use those fairy powers here in the house. I saw you the other day making all the garden tools dance through the garden doing the weeding for you. If anyone else saw that, it could be big trouble."

Annie glared back at her big brother. "Like you never use your powers? I saw you flying around the backyard as the sun was setting last night. Why do you get to use your fairy powers and not me?"

George grinned at her. "Okay, you caught me. Just be careful. That's all I'm saying. I don't fly across the school playground or make things fly across the cafeteria."

"Then I won't either," she replied.

All four placed their hands together in a pile. Zoe began, "We are brothers and sisters together as one. We use these powers only for good."

George continued, "Only for good, and sometimes a little mischief."

They all looked at George with big eyes and those fake faces of surprise and then they all laughed. A little harmless mischief never hurt as long as no one suffered.

They all jumped up and ran to get dressed. Saturday morning breakfasts were never to be missed. They were always the best. Their mom, Sara, made the yummiest pancakes with lots of gooey syrup and they always had big glasses of orange juice. The four inhaled their breakfast, thanked their mom, and dashed out the door to the big oak tree in the yard.

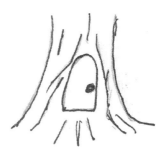

"You remember how to get to the dragon, right?"

"Yes, Zoe. We've done this several times on our own," Annie answered.

"Say hi to the dragon for me and George. Tell him we miss him and we are keeping busy."

"And tell him I'm in a big soccer game today for the championship."

Nate replied, "Okay, we'll give him your messages. Sure you don't want to come?"

Zoe told him to knock on the tree. Nate knocked three times and the magic door swung open. Annie and Nate took one more look at Zoe and George and disappeared into the tree. The door shut quietly and they were on their way down the spiral staircase to the yellow path that led to Mr. Dragon's cave.

Zoe and George smiled and looked up at the mountain. They had never quite figured out how the yellow trail reached the top of the mountain so easily, but George said it must be the dragon's magic. They both shrugged their shoulders and headed for the house. Sara greeted them at the door.

"So they are off on another adventure?"

"Yeah, sometimes I think they are lucky to be little and just starting out with the dragon. And then sometimes I am glad that I am growing up," Zoe explained. "Mr. Dragon taught me so much about myself and what I could do if I put my mind to it. I think George and I learned a lot from him."

George nodded his agreement. "I know Mr. Dragon will take good care of those twins. I just hope they don't get into any trouble. You know those twins have their own language and can do some pretty silly things."

Sara laughed. "Listen to you two. You sound like their parents."

* * * * * * *

Nate and Annie reached the dragon's doorway at the top of the yellow path and knocked on the door.

"Come on in children," the dragon answered from within. He was sitting in his rocking chair enjoying his morning newspaper and a cup of hot chocolate. "So good to see you, Nate. And how are you, Miss Annie?"

"We are great, Mr. Dragon. How are you doing?"

"I am doing well and enjoying this hot chocolate. You know Zoe introduced me to this drink and I love it. Chocolate is great!"

Nate and Annie smiled. They liked hot chocolate too and the dragon offered them each a cup. As they settled down on the sofa to sip the yummy drink, the dragon asked, "So what would you like to do today? Maybe an adventure in the Enchanted Forest? Or a trip to China?"

"Oh, Mr. Dragon, those sound like wonderful ideas. But Annie and I have been talking and we would like to visit the fairies in that chasm near Uncle Matt's house. We want to talk to the fairies and learn all about the powers that we have. We have so many questions."

"Nate, we can go there, but you must be careful. I don't want to reverse the spell and have the two of you shrink down to fairy size. Your brother and sister were not happy about that and it took a lot of work and magic to get them back. What powers do you think you have now? What are your questions? Maybe I can answer them."

Annie listed the powers that they knew about. "We know that we can point at things and move them through the air. We know we can fly. A few times I have been able to wave my hand over my milk and make it colder. I'm not sure how that works."

Nate continued, "Yeah, and I can also make things warmer by waving my hand in the opposite direction. Then there are the plants. I can point at a small seedling and it will grow really fast and even have flowers and seeds or fruit.

The other day I pointed at a small tomato plant and within minutes the plant had ripe tomatoes growing on it."

"I did the same thing with some zinnias. In just a moment, the small plants grew up and were covered with flowers. And I think I may be able to talk with animals?"

"I want to know how long we will have these powers. It's been almost five years and we don't seem to be losing them. Do you know if they will stop working?"

The dragon eyed the twins over his spectacles. "You two certainly have been experimenting and thinking about this. I think it might be better to visit the Enchanted Forest and find the green Leaf Fairy. She is very smart and should be able to answer your questions. She is like a fairy queen. Let's get ready to go."

Annie and Nate beamed at each other. They were finally going to get some answers. They packed their backpacks full of jelly sandwiches and bottles of water and climbed aboard the dragon's back. The three flew out of the cave and up into the clouds. Very soon the dragon flew down into the Enchanted Forest and landed in the central clearing. The clearing was bright with sunlight and a warm brown dirt floor. The surrounding forest was dark and it was hard to see for more than a few feet in any direction. There were several paths leading from the clearing into the woods. Each was a different glowing color. Annie and Nate knew they would venture down many of these paths on future adventures with the dragon. Today they wanted to meet the green Leaf Fairy. Which path led to her?

Mr. Dragon pointed to the pink path and said, "She is down that path. She lives in a large oak tree with golden leaves. We must approach carefully since she has several alarms set up to protect her from the leaf ants. They want to capture her and use her magic powers to make food for them."

Nate commented, "That sounds like the leaf ants in the rain forests. They collect leaves and grow their food on them."

"Something similar, Nate, but they want to steal her magic. She has alarms to scare them off and warn her if they are coming. She knows what to do to protect herself. We'll announce ourselves when we see the tree. Then we won't set off the alarms."

The three started down the glowing pink trail. Soon they saw a huge golden oak tree glowing in the dark forest. The tree was surrounded by bright sunlight and the leaves sparkled.

Mr. Dragon let out a soft and gentle roar to announce their arrival. The green Leaf Fairy flew out to meet them. She was stunningly beautiful with a flowing green gown that looked like a leaf. Her hair was the color of a brown acorn and it even looked like an acorn the way it was cut. Like all the other fairies that Nate and Annie had seen, she was about the size of a large dragonfly and she could fly about very quickly. She darted right up to the dragon's nose and sat on the tip.

"Welcome, Dragon! It has been a long time since you have visited me. It is so good to see you. How is everything and who are these young visitors you have brought?"

The dragon replied, "Hello, Leaf. It has been a long time since our last visit and I have been very well. I have brought two of my friends to meet you. This is Nate and Annie. They are two of the four children who were turned into fairies and then returned to their childhood. They have a lot of questions and they hope that you can help answer them."

Leaf flew up above Annie and Nate. "So you are two of the four who decided to return to your childhood rather than stay as fairies? I have heard that while you are children, you have many fairy qualities. Let's talk." Leaf flitted away to her tree and the three followed her. When they reached the bottom of the oak tree, they found a large bench and a table. "Have a seat and I will bring you some fairy snacks."

They sat down on the bench and the dragon smiled as Leaf disappeared into the tree. "Fairy snacks are really quite good. Leaf collects the finest honey in the forest and makes these delicious cakes. Her favorite drink is honey tea, but it is too sweet for me, so I just drink water. The water in the Enchanted Forest is so clean and fresh and cool."

Leaf returned with a large plate of little honey cakes. "Would you two like some honey tea? I know the dragon doesn't like it so I brought him some water." She put a large pitcher of glowing blue water on the table.

Annie and Nate both asked for some of the tea. "That sounds yummy. I would like to try some."

"There now, you see, Dragon. These children are willing to try new things. You should, too." Leaf giggled her fairy laugh and flew back into the tree. She returned with a tray of three cups of honey tea and a teapot. She set the tray on the table and Annie and Nate took their cups. Everyone took some honey cakes and they all settled down at the table.

"You must be Annie and Nate since the other two were older. Zoe and George? Where are they?"

Nate explained. "They are getting older and they have things to do with their friends. George is on a soccer team and he hopes to win the championship game today. They just don't seem to have the time to visit with the dragon anymore."

"My guess is they will be visiting him soon with a very serious matter. I am sensing some trouble in everyone's future, perhaps within the next three months."

Annie raised her eyebrows. "So, is that one of the things we can do with these fairy powers, predict the future?"

"We can't predict the future or know exactly what will happen, but we can feel that something good or bad, exciting or challenging will happen. Seeing you three right now, I feel that something evil is getting ready to challenge you and you will need some help to beat it back. The dragon will be in real danger and you and your brothers and sister will also be threatened. You will have to be ready."

"I have been feeling that, too," Nate said. "Something just doesn't seem right and I keep expecting some problem to happen with the dragon."

"I can't tell you what, but something is going to happen. What else do you want to know?"

Nate rested his elbows on the table. "I know I can move things with my hands, I can fly, and I can wave my hands over things and make them hot or cold. Now I know that I can sense the future. What else can I do?"

"When Zoe and George became fairies they gained all the powers of a fairy. There are so many that I can't even begin to list them all, but I have a book that will help. I'll get that for you. Your situation is unique and we honestly don't know exactly what happened. The spell changed Zoe and George back into children, but the rule since the beginning of all fairies has always been 'Once a Fairy, Always a Fairy.' The four of you will always have fairy powers, even when you grow up."

"What I don't understand is why Nate and I got the powers, too?"

"There is a very strong family bond in the fairy world. We share everything and often we know what we are doing and thinking amongst the whole group. If something really good happens to me, all of my family feels it. If someone in the family gets hurt, we all know about it. From my research through the fairy history books I think that you and Nate got the powers because you are part of Zoe and George's family, and the powers could only be passed to children since fairies are originally children and not adults."

"Wow, that is amazing!"

"Nate, there are two powers that you should know about because you will need them soon. You and your siblings can use telepathy to communicate. That means you can talk to each other through your minds without speaking. You also can locate missing things by just thinking about them and their location will pop into your head."

"I thought that Nate and I could do that because we were twins. You mean we can do the same thing with Zoe and George?"

"Your twin thing is a little different since you two can read each other's minds, and you both need to respect the other's thoughts. You can't wander into Zoe or George's thoughts and know what they are thinking. You can only talk to each other by consciously focusing on what you want to say to the other person."

The dragon was listening to the conversation and trying to take it all in. This fairy event with the four children had turned into quite a complicated mess. He wasn't sure that children could handle such powerful forces. He would need to keep an eye on them to be sure they were safe and careful.

"Can we have that book?"

"Oh, yes, Nate. Let me go get it." The Leaf Fairy flew into her tree and came out with a very small book about the size of a postage stamp. Annie and Nate stared at the tiny book.

"Uh, I don't think we are going to be able to read that small book."

"I see what you mean, Annie. I am going to make a larger copy of the book for you." The Leaf Fairy waved her hand over the tiny book and suddenly Annie was holding a regular book in her hands. "There, that should do it."

"Whoa! **All About Fairies.** Sounds like it will tell us everything we need to know. Thank you!"

"I am always here in the Enchanted Forest at my tree. If you ever need me, you can summon me by concentrating on a picture in your mind of my tree. Then we will communicate through our minds---telepathy."

The Leaf Fairy showed the three around her tree. They peeked into her house through the tiny windows. The inside of the tree was like a palace. Several fairies came by to say hello and finally it was time for the three to go home. They thanked the Leaf Fairy for all the information and the book and then climbed aboard the dragon.

"Dragon, you need to be cautious in the coming months. Someone is planning to harm you and your family. Be aware." The Leaf Fairy waved goodbye and disappeared into her tree. The three rose up through the trees and into the clouds and soon they were back at the dragon's cave.

"Time for some chocolate chip cookies and milk," the dragon said. They settled down at the big table in the dragon's kitchen for their snack.

"Thanks, Mr. Dragon, for taking us to the Leaf Fairy. We have so much to tell Zoe and George and this book is really going to help us, too."

"Yes, thank you. What did the Leaf Fairy mean about your family, Mr. Dragon? We've never heard anything about your family. What is she talking about?"

The dragon nodded his head. "I think that is a story for another day, children. It is a long one and Zoe and

George would probably like to hear it as well. Some other time."

Annie and Nate said goodbye to the dragon and raced down the yellow path to the spiral staircase. When they reached the top they burst into the yard and ran to the back door. As they came into the kitchen, Sara and Jim were sitting with Zoe and George enjoying an afternoon snack. The twins slid into their seats and started racing through their adventure in the Enchanted Forest. They showed everyone the fairy book.

"Slow down there, you two. Let me get my journal so I can write this down." Sara reached up to the top shelf in one of the cabinets and found her journal. She settled at the table with her pen and began to record the twins' story. There was a lot to write.

Ha Ha

Chapter 2

<u>The Box of Chuckles</u>

The loud clap of thunder woke the twins. It was the first Saturday morning in July and summer thunderstorms often shook their window. They jumped out of bed and ran to the window to see the storm.

"Look at those big black clouds in the morning sunlight. The storm is coming over the mountain and the sun is rising in front of the house so the sunlight is shining on the clouds. It is so beautiful."

Then a bright flash of lightning dashed across the sky and hit the top of the mountain, followed by a loud clap of thunder. George and Zoe came flying into the room to see the storm.

"Pretty big storm coming. We better make sure all the windows are closed." Zoe squinted her eyes shut and talked out loud. "Living room is good, dining room, kitchen, den, all four bedrooms. I think we are okay." She had just used one of her fairy powers to check the whole house. The four had learned a lot about their powers in the fairy book that Leaf had given Annie.

"That is pretty cool, Zoe." She grinned at Annie and said thanks. The four sat in the window and watched the storm pass over the mountaintop. They knew the dragon was safely snuggled away in his cave. Their stomachs began to growl for breakfast so they got dressed and headed down to the kitchen. Sara had prepared a scrumptious breakfast of pancakes, fresh blueberries, lots of gooey syrup, and large glasses of orange juice. Jim joined the family and everyone settled down at the table.

"So what are our adventurers up to today? Can the dragon make the rain go away?" he asked.

"I think the storm will pass by soon and it will be a sunny day." Zoe and George were both going to the swim team practice. They were getting ready for the first swim meet next week. George loved to do the backstroke and Zoe's favorite was freestyle. Zoe could beat everyone while George was usually in the middle of the group. It was good exercise and they enjoyed being with their friends at the pool all day.

Nate and Annie were planning on visiting the dragon. They hugged their mom and dad goodbye and raced across the yard to the big oak tree, knocked three times, and the little door opened. They climbed inside and slid down the railing of the spiral staircase to the yellow pathway below. They dashed up the path to the dragon's doorway and knocked on the doorframe.

"Come in, children. How are things going with your family?"

"Everything is terrific, Mr. Dragon. Zoe and George are going to their swim team practice. We're here for a big adventure today. Where shall we go?"

"I need to deliver some of my garden vegetables to an old friend in the Rocky Mountains. Would you like to go along?"

"Wow, the Rocky Mountains," Nate exclaimed. "I would love to go see them. George talks about them all the time when we see the snow skiing on the TV. They are big mountains."

"Yes Nate, they are big mountains out west. So let's get on our way." Annie and Nate packed their backpacks with lots of peanut butter sandwiches and bottles of water. They thought it would be a long trip and they would need a lot of supplies. The dragon also handed them a big backpack of vegetables. They hopped aboard the dragon's back and flew out of the cave. The three passed through the clouds and soon came to the majestic Rocky Mountains, snow covered on the top with rushing rivers and the plains below at their base.

"How cool is that!" exclaimed Annie. "Can we play in the snow in the middle of the summer?"

The dragon flew to the top of one of the mountains and landed in a snowy field. "We can stay here a few minutes until you get cold and then we can fly down to meet my friend." Nate and Annie ran across the snow field. In the warm air they could roll around in the snow without freezing. They threw snowballs at each other and even made a snowman. After about twenty minutes, Annie said she had had enough and Nate agreed. They were ready to meet the dragon's friend. The twins climbed aboard the dragon and glided down the face of the mountain to the valley below. They landed in a beautiful sunlit meadow full of beautiful flowers.

They found a nice sunny spot to eat their picnic lunch. The peanut butter and jelly tasted so good after playing in the snow. "We should have made some hot chocolate," Annie joked. "Hot chocolate in the summertime? Ha!" The sun was so warm and the three rested on a big flat rock and fell asleep. After a time, they were awakened by a loud horn blaring from the nearby forest. They all sat up.

"What was that?"

"That is my friend, Sir John. He is a good knight and I always bring him the fresh vegetables from my garden." The dragon pointed at the backpack full of vegetables. "Many years ago I saved him from a very mean dragon who wanted to burn him up. I protected him from the fiery dragon's breath and then sent the mean dragon away. We have been friends ever since."

Nate laughed. "That's a real switch on the old fairy tales. Usually the dragon and the knight are enemies and have a big fight."

Mr. Dragon raised an eyebrow at Nate. "And the dragon almost always ends up on the wrong end of the knight's sword, Nate."

Nate bowed his head and sheepishly replied, "I'm sorry for bringing that up, Mr. Dragon. It is just a story."

The dragon reached over and patted Nate on the head. "Don't worry, Nate. Those are mostly just stories and I am glad that Sir John and I are close friends."

The three looked across the meadow and saw a large red fox running out of the forest. He was almost as big as the dragon and Annie and Nate had never seen such a large fox. The fox was running on two legs carrying a pointed stick in one front paw and a golden box in the other paw. He was running really fast right at them.

"What is he carrying?"

"That red fox is always up to no good. The golden box is the knight's prized treasure of chuckles that he has collected over the years. When he goes somewhere on a trip, he collects the laughter that he hears around him. Then he can open the box at home and enjoy the laughter again. It always cheers him up and I am sure he is not happy that the red fox has taken it. We must stop the fox and return the box to Sir John."

As the fox approached, the dragon stood up on the rock. He roared at the fox, "You must return the box, Red Fox. It is not yours to keep."

The fox looked the dragon straight in the eye. "And who put you in charge, Dragon? If I want this box, I'll keep it. So there."

The dragon stepped in front of the fox to stop him. The fox took his sharp stick and stabbed the dragon's foot. The dragon was so surprised that he fell down and the fox ran off across the field. Sir John came charging out of the forest on his white horse and galloped over to the dragon and the children.

"Oh my, Dragon. That crafty old fox has stabbed you in the foot. I must help you, so he can keep the box. I will find another." The knight jumped off of his horse and went to the dragon. The stick was lodged between two of the dragon's claws and it hurt a lot. The dragon was groaning and holding his foot.

Annie turned to the knight. "Sir John, I am Annie and this is Nate. We are friends of the dragon, too. You fix his foot and we are going to catch the fox and bring back the box." Before the knight could say anything, Annie and Nate flew into the air and raced across the meadow after the fox.

As the fox ran into the trees, Annie and Nate caught up to him. He didn't even know they were behind him until they each grabbed one of his ears. Annie and Nate lifted the fox off the ground and carried him high into one of the trees. They dropped him on a branch and Nate grabbed the box from the fox. Annie and Nate flew a safe distance away from the stunned fox who was clinging to the branch.

"Where did you two children come from? Give me back my box and get me down out of this tree!" the fox demanded. Nate glared at the fox and held the box tightly against his chest.

"Now see here, Red Fox," Annie began. "We know this box belongs to the knight and you stole it. What is even worse, you hurt our dragon when you stuck him with your pointy stick. He has a sliver between his toes and that is not nice."

The fox was not a happy camper. "If I want that box, I can take it. Finders keepers and all that. That old knight doesn't need it. He is always laughing so he doesn't need any more chuckles. I need some laughs because my life is so miserable." Then the fox made a sad face and tried to trick Annie and Nate. He shed fake tears and sobbed, "My life is so miserable. No one visits me and I have to catch my food in the forest. It isn't easy being a fox," he cried loudly.

Nate looked at Annie. "Such a clever fox, Annie. Too bad for him that I can read his mind. He is making it all up. He has a large den deep in the forest where he collects all the things that he steals from people. He just wanted to add the gold box to his collection. I think he can sit on that branch for a while and think about what a naughty fox he is."

The fox became really angry. "Listen to me, you wretched little boy. You can't leave me here in this tree. I stabbed your dragon with a poisoned stick and he will get really sick and probably die if you don't take me back to save him. I will take the box as payment for saving his life."

Annie turned to Nate. "Time for us to go. This clever fox is now beginning to lie too much. The stick hurt the dragon, but it did not have any poison on it, Fox. One too many lies has done you in. I am guessing it will take you a long time to get down out of this tree. And it serves you right. Leave the knight alone."

Annie and Nate turned and flew out of the forest back to the knight and the dragon. When they reached the rock, the knight had already pulled out the big sliver of wood from the dragon's claw.

"It went pretty deep but lucky for the dragon I always carry my first aid kit. I pulled out the sliver with my trusty tweezers and then I cleaned the wound with some alcohol. Then I put some healing salve on the wound and wrapped it in a bandage. Quite good at this doctoring thing, I think." The knight smiled and looked very proud. The dragon let out a laugh and rolled his eyes.

"You are such a good friend to come to my aid. Thank you, John."

"Ah, I see you found my golden box of chuckles. How did you ever get it back from the fox?"

Nate and Annie told the knight and the dragon what they had done to the fox. The dragon nodded his approval. "Those fairy powers are coming in quite handy. In the old days, your brother and sister would have had to chase the fox and trap him in some way. Good job."

The knight eyed the two children suspiciously. "Just exactly how can you fly? That doesn't seem natural to me. Are you sure you aren't wizards or something evil that I must be careful of?"

The children giggled. "I wish we had those pointy hats like wizards," Nate said. "We are related to the fairies and we got our powers from them. So we are not evil. We are the dragon's friends."

"Any friend of the dragon is a friend of mine. Thank you for retrieving my golden box full of chuckles. Why don't you come to the castle for a bit of a snack?"

The four walked through the forest to the knight's castle. They enjoyed a yummy snack and then the twins spent the afternoon exploring the castle while the dragon and the knight talked. Then it was time to fly home. They climbed aboard the dragon and waved goodbye to the knight. They flew through the clouds and arrived back at the dragon's cave in no time.

"Oh my, it is a bit late, children. You need to run on home and tell your mother that I am sorry we are late."

"We will let her know about our great adventure. See you soon."

Annie and Nate ran down the yellow path and up the spiral staircase. They opened the door in the tree and scurried across the backyard to the kitchen door. Sara met them at the door. "Everything okay?"

"Yeah, sorry we are late. The dragon had some trouble with a big red fox and we had to save him."

Sara settled down at the kitchen table with her journal. "That old red fox. He is just so bad. Tell me all about it."

Chapter 3

<u>The Toothless Dragon</u>

In the middle of summer vacation all the days seem like the weekend. This hot and humid Tuesday morning Gib was coming over for a visit. Gib's family had moved into the farm next door several years ago right before Gib was born. His older sister, Camille, was Zoe's best friend. Nate and Annie had met Gib a few times at parties but they had never had him come over for a playdate. Today would be the beginning of a new friendship for the three five-year-olds. Nate and Annie jumped out of bed, got dressed, and ran down to breakfast.

Sara had prepared one of their favorite breakfasts--- oatmeal with blueberries and dates mixed in. As they gobbled down their food, Sara told them that she had received a letter from Zoe. George, Zoe, and Camille were away at a sleepover summer camp for a week.

Sara read the letter to Annie and Nate. Then the three talked about Gib and meeting the dragon. "Is it okay for Gib to meet him?"

"I think so. Since Camille has known the dragon for years, I don't see why Gib can't meet the dragon, too. You will need to take some time as you play this morning to talk about the dragon. Tell him what the dragon looks like and that he is friendly. I think that Gib will be just fine with visiting the dragon."

Gib and his mom, Jessica, arrived about an hour later. Sara told Jessica she would bring Gib home in the afternoon around four o'clock. Jessica thanked her and gave Gib a big hug. "See you later, buddy. Have fun with Nate and Annie."

Nate, Annie, and Gib played in the backyard for a while, kicking a ball around and exploring all of Sara's gardens. They showed Gib her big vegetable garden and Gib named many of the plants. His mom also had a big garden and Sara and Jessica shared plants back and forth. The three went on playing with the ball. When the ball hit the big oak tree, Annie turned to Gib and asked, "Hey Gib, do you want to meet our dragon? He is really friendly and he takes us on adventures all over the world."

Gib replied, "Yeah, sure, why not? It sounds like a lot of fun. Where is he?" Gib looked around the yard.

Nate explained that the dragon lived on top of Sugarloaf Mountain. Gib looked up at the mountain and said he was ready to meet the dragon but it looked like a long walk. Annie ran inside to tell her mom where they were going. Sara came out to the tree.

"Hi Gib. So do you think you would like to meet the dragon?" He nodded. Sara continued, "Great! You must understand that most people don't believe in the dragon. You can tell your mom about him, but she probably won't believe you. Very few adults can see him or know anything about him. Camille met the dragon a few years back with Zoe and George. She told your mom, but your mom said that there were no such things as dragons. So don't be upset if she doesn't believe you about the dragon."

Gib replied, "So the dragon really exists? Camille talks about him all the time and Mom always tells her the dragon is imaginary. Camille always smiles. She knows the dragon?"

"Yes, George and Zoe took her to meet him years ago and she often goes on adventures with them. I think she will be pleased that you met the dragon and know about him, too."

"All right! I'm ready to go meet the famous dragon. How do we get to his cave? Up that trail?"

Sara patted the twins on their heads. "Annie and Nate will teach you all about him. I'll leave you all to your adventures. Have fun!" Sara walked back to the kitchen door. She stood on the porch and watched as Nate knocked on the tree three times and the doorway opened. The three disappeared into the tree and the little door shut. They were off to see the dragon.

Gib was a brave little guy and he was amazed by the spiral staircase and the yellow path. He ran along with Nate and Annie up to the dragon's door. Nate knocked on the doorframe and the dragon invited them in.

"Good morning, children. I see you have brought a new friend." The dragon smiled at Gib and Gib knew at once that this dragon was good.

"Hi. My name is Gib and I think you know my sister Camille."

"Ah, Camille's little brother. How nice to meet you, Gib. Camille talks about you all the time. She will be very happy to know that you have joined our group. If you have any questions, please let me know. And what would you all like to do today?"

Annie and Nate smiled at Gib and then they said in unison, "Candy Land".

The dragon raised his eyebrows in surprise. "Candy Land? And what might you know about Candy Land?"

Annie explained, "We play the board game with Zoe and George all the time and Zoe once said that Candy Land was a real place. She said you took them there."

"Ah yes, I remember that adventure. Seems like a good idea. Let's get ready."

Annie and Nate showed Gib how to pack for the trip. They were surprised to find a backpack already hanging on a hook marked "Gib". Did the dragon know they would bring Gib?

The three children climbed aboard the dragon's back and flew out of the cave. Gib was thrilled with the ride and pointed to his house in the distance. They rose into the clouds and then came out over a glowing green island in the middle of a big blue ocean. They descended and landed in a large field.

"Is this Candy Land?" they asked.

The dragon chuckled and explained that Candy Land was on this island, but they would have to hike across the meadow and over a hill to reach the candy factory. Nate took the lead and Annie, Gib, and the dragon followed. As they crested the hill they saw a huge amusement park before them filled with children playing. They ran down the hill to the park entrance where a tall clown greeted them.

"Welcome to Candy Land where you can eat all the candy you want. Come on in and have some fun!"

The dragon knew that Candy Land was a trap for young children. With free candy and free amusement rides, children could get lost in their dreams and forget about leaving. This would be a good lesson for Annie, Nate, and Gib. He watched as the three children dashed into the park and began collecting all kinds of candy. When their arms were full, they found a picnic table and spread out all of their loot.

"Look at the size of this chocolate bar! Yum, yum!"

"What about these gum balls? They will last all day." Annie stuffed several into her pockets.

"These lollipops are my favorites. I'll take some home for Camille."

After eating several pieces of candy, the three children were groaning from too much. But they wanted to go on the rides, so the dragon followed them through the park. "First let's go on the boat ride. Then we can climb on the ropes. And then we can go on the roller coaster."

Annie told Nate she didn't like his ideas. He needed to do what she wanted to do. Then Gib started yelling at both of them about what he wanted to do. They got into quite an argument and then they saw the dragon watching them.

"Wait a minute!" Annie exclaimed. "We don't fight like this. We never argue over little things like some amusement park rides. What's going on?"

"You're right, Annie. I am sorry I was so mean to you. What is going on? Why do we feel this way?"

Gib turned to them. "It's the candy. When I eat a lot of candy I get really mean with Camille. My mom makes me take a timeout. A little bit of candy is okay, but too much sugar just isn't good for your body. We need to stop eating this stuff."

"But I can't," Nate whined. "It's just too good!" He ate another chocolate bar before Annie could stop him.

"Nate, give me that candy right now! You have to stop."

Nate glared at Annie and ran away from the table. "Oh dear, Gib, what are we going to do? Nate won't listen."

Annie and Gib left all their candy on the table and ran after Nate. He dodged through the crowd and ran into a big dark cave. Annie and Gib followed. The dragon was watching from the shadows. Annie and Gib groped through the darkness until they bumped into Nate.

"What are you doing, Nate?"

"Look at those big red eyes, Annie! We need to get out of here."

They saw the big red eyes glowing in the dark and then the lights came on. They were temporarily blinded by the light and then they were able to focus on a scrawny dragon lying on the floor. He raised his head a little and smiled a weak smile. All of his teeth were rotten and he could barely speak.

In a weak little voice he said, "I am so glad you came back to save me. Zoe, George, Camille, it has been so long since I last saw you. Please save me like you did last time."

The three children looked at each other. How did this dragon know their brother and sisters? What was wrong with him? What did he mean they needed to save him?

Annie stepped forward. "Hello. My name is Annie and this is Nate and Gib. We are the brothers and sister of Zoe, George, and Camille. How can we help you?"

The dragon raised his head a little and spoke slowly. "Can I have some water? The candy has made me so weak. I cannot find water." Gib and Nate searched the room and found a large barrel of water nearby. They scooped some water into a cup and brought it to the dragon.

"Ah, my first drink in such a long time." The dragon's voice grew stronger. "You see, Candy Land is a trap to capture children and keep them here forever. The evil clown gives the children all the candy they want and in return he puts them to work in his candy factories. They are prisoners.

"I tried to warn the children and the evil clown chained me to this post in this dark warehouse. Since I couldn't brush my teeth or drink any water, all of my teeth rotted from the candy. You must free the children."

Nate shook his head. "That candy really is bad for your head. We need to figure out what to do. Annie…Gib…what do you think?"

The three sat down with the poor dragon. "First we need to free this dragon. Then we need to do something with that clown. And then we need to free the children."

"But where will they go? How do we capture that clown?"

Gib outlined a plan that Annie and Nate both liked. "Okay, let's find some tools and break this chain so the dragon is free. Will you be able to help us once you are free?"

The dragon nodded his head. "Once the chain is broken, my magical powers will return. Then I can take care of the clown. I'll put a spell on him and lock him in a cage."

"Then the last thing we need to do is free the children from this candy craze."

Nate found a tool chest in the corner and brought over a hammer and chisel. "Here, I can break the chain with this." Gib found a rusty link and together they pounded on the chain until it broke. The sickly dragon began to change color and look much healthier. His teeth grew and he had a new shining smile. He stood up and waved his wings.

"Okay dragon, you need to get rid of that clown. Nate, you turn off the power and all the rides will stop working. Gib, you and I are going to use that big fire hose outside the doorway to wash down all the candy and melt it. Without all the sugar, the children will start to see what is happening. But I am afraid that I have no idea what to do with the children once they are free."

The children's dragon stepped forward out of the shadows. "You have done well figuring this out. First you recognized the danger. Then you found this poor dragon and freed him. Your plan to destroy the candy and close the park is a very good one. Once the children are free, I will take care of them and send them home."

The dragon from the warehouse bowed to Mr. Dragon. "It is so good of you to return. Thank you, friend." The warehouse dragon left to capture the clown. Nate left to find the power box. Annie and Gib stood by the fire hose waiting for everything to happen. There was a loud clap of thunder and the warehouse dragon flew out of the sky and grabbed the clown. The clown tried to fight the dragon but he was too strong and threw the clown into a cage, slamming and locking the door. Then all the rides stopped working and all the children stood still. Nate had found the power switch and turned off everything in the park. The music stopped and all the lights went out.

The children began to whine and cry, "What has happened to our park? We want more candy."

Annie and Gib turned on the fire hose and soaked the children. The water dissolved all the candy and the children began to look around.

"What am I doing here?"

"Where is my family?"

"I want to go home."

Annie, Nate, and Gib stepped forward. "Listen, everyone! You have been under the clown's magic spell. He has kept you here as prisoners using the candy to trap you. We have captured the clown and turned off all the rides and washed away the candy. You are now free. Our dragon will take care of you."

Mr. Dragon spread his wings and told the children to hold out their arms like wings. Then he said "Home Sweet Home" three times and the children began to rise into the air and disappear into the clouds. Soon all the captured children were gone. Mr. Dragon turned to the warehouse dragon and said, "You are in charge now. I will leave the clown to you. Remember that he has tricked you before. Don't let him do that again. We are returning home."

"Thank you for saving me again and for freeing the children. This time I will take care of this clown. He won't trick me again. Have a safe trip home."

Nate, Annie, and Gib climbed aboard the dragon's back and flew up into the clouds. Soon they arrived back at the dragon's cave. They settled down around the dragon's kitchen table for some cookies and milk.

Gib exclaimed, "Wow! That was a real adventure! Amazing, simply amazing."

They talked more about what had happened and then it was time to go. The children waved goodbye to the dragon and Gib gave the dragon a big hug. "Thanks for including me."

The three ran down the yellow path, up the staircase, and out into the yard. They sprinted to the back door and burst into the kitchen. "You won't believe what happened to us today!" they all shouted. Sara got her journal and pen and sat at the table.

"I'm ready to hear it all."

Chapter 4

Janey's Trap

It was a Saturday morning in late July. The sun shone brightly and the humidity was heavy in the air. Annie and Nate jumped out of bed and flew over to the window. "The dragon's cave will be cool on this hot and humid morning. Let's see what adventures we can go on today." They got dressed and slid down the banister to breakfast in the kitchen. George and his father had eaten early and they had already left on their fishing trip for the day. Zoe had spent the night at Camille's house and she was coming home shortly.

"Gib is coming with Zoe, so if you guys want to wait a few minutes, maybe he can go with you to the dragon's cave," Sara said.

"Sure, Mom. It's great to have Gib along. We call ourselves the Three Caballeros after that Disney cartoon we saw. Nate and I are the two parrots and Gib is Donald Duck. He can even talk like Donald. The dragon thinks it is pretty funny!"

"And Gib has some really good ideas when we all need to think up solutions to the dragon's problems. I think he might grow up to be an inventor or something like that."

"I'm glad you three have so much fun together. He should be here soon."

Sara finished up the breakfast dishes while Nate and Annie played their Candy Land game. They talked about the mean clown and the brave warehouse dragon that saved everyone. They hoped that all the children had found their way to their homes.

They heard the car drive up to the house and the doors slam. Zoe brought Gib into the house and the Three Caballeros were off on their next adventure. Nate led the way with Annie and Gib in close pursuit. They reached the tree, knocked three times, and the little door opened. Down the stairs and up the path, they arrived at the dragon's doorway in no time. Gib knocked on the doorframe.

"Come on in, children. How is everyone today? It is a little hot and humid out there. Maybe we should just stay here in the cave and read books today."

"Hey, Mr. Dragon. We are doing great and we can stand the heat. We want to go out and explore the world. Where should we go?"

Nate explained that he had been watching a show on television about farming in Ohio. He thought it sounded really interesting and they should go visit one of the farms.

Gib said, "I've never been to Ohio. Is it a nice place?"

Annie chimed in, "We haven't been there either, Gib. I guess we are going to find out, if it is okay with Mr. Dragon."

"All right, children, Ohio it is. Let's get ready to go." The three got busy packing their backpacks with plenty of water for the hot day and some sandwiches for lunch. They climbed onto the dragon's back and flew up into the clouds. As they rose, the hot air cooled and it was refreshing to be in the clouds.

"Maybe we could spend the day up here. It is so nice and cool," Annie shouted. Everyone laughed.

Soon they descended out of the clouds and down into a vast farmland. As far as they could see there were fields of corn. There were some barns and farmhouses dotted about the countryside. Nate pointed to a big white house and red barn with a tall silo. "Let's go there."

The dragon glided across the cornfield towards the big red barn. He landed in the barnyard near the pigpens. "P-U! This place really stinks!" Annie giggled. The three pinched their noses to keep out the strong odor. The dragon led them around to the front of the barn. They found a girl about their age sitting on an old tractor watching the birds fly into a big tree.

The girl turned and saw the three children and the dragon. "Holy cow! I just knew that dragons existed! I just knew it! I was just thinking how lucky those birds were to fly and how a dragon could teach me how to fly and then you appeared. Holy cow!" The girl then spoke to Annie, Nate, and Gib. "And where did you three come from?"

"We flew here on the dragon's back. We live in Maryland. I'm Nate, this is Annie and Gib."

The girl jumped down off of the tractor and walked over to meet them. "My name is Janey and I live here on this farm with my mom and dad. They are busy with their morning chores and I was just getting ready to feed the hogs. You want to help?" Janey kept her eye on the dragon while she talked to the Three Caballeros.

"Yeah, that sounds like fun! What do we do?" Janey showed the three how to take buckets of food scraps and feed over to the pigpen and dump the contents into the trough. Then she took them into the barn making sure that the dragon followed them.

"So tell me about your dragon. Can he talk? Is he dangerous? Did you train him? Is he your pet?"

The three laughed and Annie explained. "No, Mr. Dragon is our friend. He is so nice and very clever and he takes us all over the world on adventures. We first met him on Sugarloaf Mountain near our house. He has a cave there and we visit him all the time. He has all kinds of magical powers." The three children stood next to the dragon hugging his legs.

"Holy cow! So you can talk, Mr. Dragon?"

Mr. Dragon replied, "It is a pleasure to meet you, Janey. Do you know much about dragons?"

"I've read so many books and my uncle lives in Maryland and he does research on dragons so he has taught me a lot about them. He said that if I could catch a dragon I could be really famous. I don't suppose you have any friends that would want to be my dragon?"

"I can ask the other dragons if they are interested, Janey. What else can you tell us about your farm?" They all sat down on bales of hay inside the barn and Janey explained how they planted and harvested corn with giant machines. She told them about her vegetable garden where she raised the family's food. Janey talked about the cows and pigs that they raised. Then she offered to get everyone some lemonade.

"Oh, that sounds yummy! I am pretty thirsty from this heat," Nate said.

"Thank you, Janey. I think some lemonade would be delicious," the dragon said.

Janey stared at the dragon again. "You like lemonade? I thought dragons just drank blood. Hmmm, I'm learning a lot about dragons."

"People have many strange ideas about dragons from the many years of fairy tales and stories that have been told. Most everything you read in the books is just not true," Nate explained.

Gib joined in. "Yeah, I just met the dragon a few weeks ago. He is so cool and friendly. We do all kinds of things together."

"Okay, I'll be right back. You all just stay inside the barn and everything will be just fine." Janey left the barn and closed the door behind her.

"She seems like a nice girl. It must be tough living on a farm out here with no neighbors or friends. Sounds like she reads a lot," Annie noted.

"What did she mean 'everything will be just fine'? That sounded kind of funny," Gib said.

As they sat on the bales of hay waiting for Janey to return, they noticed that the barn was gradually getting darker. "Seems like it must be getting cloudy or something. It's getting pretty dark in here." Then they realized that someone had been closing the shutters on the barn, one by one, very quietly. "That seems really odd. Why would anyone want to close the shutters like that?"

Then they heard a big clunk at the barn door and they realized that someone had locked the barn door from outside. They could hear Janey talking to someone.

"I did it, Uncle Thor. I've captured a dragon in our barn! I finally have my own pet dragon. Holy cow! Now what am I supposed to do with it?"

The Three Caballeros and the dragon realized what had happened. Janey had been closing and locking all the shutters and the barn door so they could not escape. "Mr. Dragon, what are we going to do? She wants to keep you here locked up in this barn."

The dragon replied, "Maybe we can talk with her and explain things to her."

They could hear Janey still talking. "Uncle Thor, you can get here in two hours in your private plane? And you can help me train the dragon? Oh, I can't wait to see you. Hurry!"

"That doesn't sound good, Mr. Dragon," Nate said. "I think we better find a way out of this barn so we can get home." Annie and Gib agreed. "All right, Gib. You must swear that you will never tell anyone what you are going to see now."

Gib had a confused look on his face. "I swear I won't tell anyone, but what am I going to see?"

"Gib, we have magic powers that we got from some fairies. We are going to use our powers to escape, but you can't tell anyone about it or we will get in big trouble. Do you swear?"

Gib crossed his heart with his arms and then spit in his hand. "I swear Annie. I won't tell anyone, but I want to fly, too!"

"Can't do that right now. We can talk with the Leaf Fairy later."

Annie and Nate flew up into the rafters of the barn. They looked everywhere for any opening. Nate found an open window on the second floor. He could see Janey walking across the barnyard towards her farmhouse. He told Annie that he would open the door and then everyone should be ready to fly out. Annie went below to tell Gib and the dragon.

Nate waited until Janey was on her porch. Then he flew out the window and down to the barn door. He lifted the latch and moved the heavy log that was leaning against the door, and then he pulled the door open. "Let's go!"

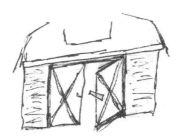

Annie and Gib were already on the dragon's back and Nate flew up and joined them. Then they all flew out the barn door. Janey saw them swoosh over the barnyard and she ran off the porch yelling at them.

"Hey, you come back! You are my dragon now! I captured you! You need to mind me! I'm your trainer. I'm your owner!"

Annie leaned out over the dragon's back and yelled down to Janey. "Nobody owns Mr. Dragon! And you are the one who needs some training in good manners!"

Then the dragon and the three children disappeared into the clouds. Janey pulled out her cell phone and called her Uncle Thor. She was in tears. "Uncle Thor, he escaped. There were three children with him and they freed him from the barn. They said he lived on Sugarloaf Mountain somewhere in Maryland. I want my dragon back. Please help me, Uncle Thor!"

The dragon flew down out of the clouds and landed in his cave. The three children climbed off of his back. "Thank you, children, for rescuing me! That was really terrible. It is so sad when people want to trap dragons. She had some strange ideas about dragons. I hope we never have to see her again."

Annie said, "I can't imagine why she would think you were some kind of a pet that needed to be trained and locked up. And thinking that you drink blood! That is just plain disgusting."

The four settled down at the dragon's table and had cookies and milk. They talked more about the trip and the little girl. "Who do you think this Thor guy is? I wonder if he lives around here?"

The dragon raised his eyebrows as if he knew something, but then he just said, "I am glad that adventure is over. You all did some great thinking there."

Gib spoke up. "I want some of those fairy powers! I want to fly and do all that magic stuff."

The dragon smiled at Gib. "Gib, the children have their fairy powers because of a magic accident. We really don't know how it happened. We can talk with the Leaf

Fairy, but I am not sure you can have fairy powers and remain a child."

"I can't wait to visit the Enchanted Forest again and talk with Leaf."

"We will talk with her, but I can't promise anything, Gib."

They finished up their snack and headed down the path towards home. They climbed the stairs and darted across the lawn to the kitchen. Before they entered the house, Annie turned to Gib.

"My mom knows that we have these fairy powers, but she mustn't know that you do. So remember, you can't tell anyone about this."

"I swear, Annie. Nobody will know from me."

Sara greeted them and wrote down the adventure in her book. She was concerned that someone in Maryland might know about dragons. She wondered who Uncle Thor was. She would keep on guard just in case.

THE AMERICAN MUSEUM OF

MAGIC AND MYTHS

Chapter 5

A Surprising Field Trip

It was a warm September morning and the sun was shining brightly. Everyone was going to school today. Zoe and Camille were in eighth grade, George was entering seventh, and it was Nate, Annie, and Gib's first year in kindergarten. The three little ones were enjoying each day at school while George was busy studying so many new things. Zoe and Camille were working really hard at their studies as well as exploring friendships and even a school dance with some boys. They were growing up way too fast.

Zoe was going on a field trip today. Her English class was studying fairy tales and how adults used them to teach their children to behave. She was enjoying this unit since so many of the stories were about dragons, unicorns, fairies, and magic. She and Camille would share knowing smiles when the teacher would say that all this was make-believe and dragons and fairies were just imaginary characters. Today's field trip was to a local Museum of Magic and Myths to meet a scientist who was conducting research on whether dragons really existed and where the idea had started. There were several exhibits at the museum about medieval England and Germany where many of the fairy tales had started. Zoe and Camille were interested to see how all this would be presented.

When the class arrived at the museum, the students were given a sheet with ten questions. The teacher explained the assignment. "You will have one hour to tour the museum on your own and find the answers to these ten questions. We will meet at eleven o'clock sharp in the lecture hall over there. See you in an hour."

The students scattered and Zoe and Camille started with an exhibit on wizards and black magic. An hour later, they had found the answers to all ten questions and they headed for the lecture hall. Both girls knew that a lot of the information they had found was wrong. For example, the dragon exhibit said that dragons only drank human blood and ate live goats. Zoe knew that was not true. Camille had found an exhibit about fairies that said they were always irresponsible and selfish. She knew for a fact that Zoe and George were not that way. But Camille and Zoe agreed that they didn't have any way to prove that the exhibits were wrong so they would just keep their thoughts to themselves. It was best if people didn't believe in the dragon and just left him alone.

The students settled into their seats in the lecture hall and their teacher introduced Professor Thor Grimmstone. Camille guessed that he was probably in his late thirties about the same age as her parents. Dressed in a black suit with a white shirt and tie, he was tall and thin. His eyes were dark and piercing and he did not seem very friendly.

Two students entered the room just a moment too late and he yelled at them and embarrassed them for not being on time. They quickly sat down in the back row.

Professor Grimmstone paced back and forth behind his table staring at the students. Then he turned and faced them. His eyes were open wide and he looked like a wild man. "So you think you know all about dragons and magic? You know nothing. I have spent my whole life studying these nasty lizards. Even though most people think they are imaginary, I know otherwise. They are evil. They are dangerous.   They are real! They will take over the world if we don't stop them.

"I am on the verge of discovering a real live dragon and I will soon have him in a cage for all to see. I have spies, I have information, I know things. After years of searching, I have found a spell book lost in the archives of the New York City Library. There is a spell that I will cast on the dragon when I find him that will take away his magic powers. It will extinguish his fiery breath. Then I will capture him and take him to a zoo for everyone to see. I will be the famous dragon catcher and all the world will know of me."

The professor went on for another ten minutes describing all the details he had learned about dragons. While most of the students were chuckling and looking at each other with grins, Zoe and Camille listened intently as the professor described many of their dragon's habits. He clearly knew some true things about dragons. All of their classmates were whispering about this crazy man and using their fingers to make circles around their heads like he was nuts. Even their teacher was beginning to wonder if it was a mistake to let the professor continue to preach about the dragons. She tried to interrupt him but he waved her aside and continued.

Camille and Zoe were busy taking notes and listening to every word. "This man is dangerous," Zoe whispered to Camille. "He knows far too much about dragons. We will need to find out about this spell book and what he is up to."

Camille nodded in agreement. "We need to tell George and the others and then get to the dragon and warn him. Maybe he knows about the spell book. This does not sound good, Zoe. We must protect Mr. Dragon."

The professor ended his speech by pointing his finger at the students and shouting, "You will see! I am the dragon catcher! I will get the evil lizard and put him in a cage. Mark my words. Before we reach Halloween I will have him." Then the professor turned and disappeared through a doorway. The sign on the door said: Dragon Catcher.

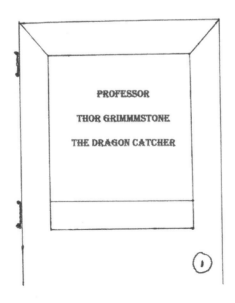

PROFESSOR

THOR GRIMMMSTONE

THE DRAGON CATCHER

As soon as he left the room, everyone started talking. The teacher had to raise her voice to get the students to settle down. "Now, children, I think the professor really believes that he is right, even though we know that this is all just a bunch of fairy tales and stories. He certainly makes you feel like there are dragons. I think we will discuss his ideas more in class tomorrow. Now it's time to board the bus to head back to school. Please line up at the door."

Everyone collected their belongings and lined up near the exit. Zoe and Camille could hear many conversations about the nutty professor and his crazy ideas. Who could possibly believe in dragons? The students couldn't wait to share this experience with their families and friends. While everyone seemed convinced that the professor was out of his mind, Zoe and Camille knew otherwise. They would be sharing all they heard with Sara and Jim. The bus ride back to school was long and difficult as the students continued their mockery of the professor.

As soon as school was out, Zoe and Camille rode the bus to Zoe's house and ran all the way down the lane to the farmhouse. They burst into the kitchen as Sara was taking a cake out of the oven. She could tell they were upset. "What is the matter? You look like you've seen a ghost."

"Much worse than a ghost, Mom. Mr. Dragon is in danger and we have a big problem on our hands."

Sara set the cake on the counter to cool and moved to the kitchen table. "Tell me what you have learned." The girls told Sara everything from their trip. Sara took notes in her journal so they could remember every detail.

"We will need to tell the family and then let the dragon know. This does not sound good. Something is very wrong."

Zoe added, "My fairy powers tell me that the professor is telling the truth and I can sense something really bad is going to happen soon. We need to get ready."

Chapter 6

<u>Family Meeting on the Mountain</u>

During the family meeting, George proposed that Zoe and Camille should return to the museum and try to get into the lab. Maybe they could find the spell book and take it to the dragon. As much as they wanted to help the dragon, Sara and Jim were not in favor of any of their children sneaking around a museum stealing things. George pointed out that the professor had already stolen the book from the library so Zoe and Camille would be taking it back to return it to the library.

"George, I realize that you want to protect the dragon and you are right that the book is stolen property. But I cannot allow my children to be involved in anything like a robbery and if Zoe and Camille were caught it would appear to be a robbery regardless of what we might know. No sneaking into the museum or taking the book, at least not yet." Jim was firm about this so George accepted his dad's directions.

Nate asked, "Don't you think we need to at least tell the dragon?"

Zoe replied, "That's a good idea, Nate. You and Annie and Gib should tell him about Thor Grimmstone. He might know something."

"Wait a minute," Annie said. "We were in Ohio at a farm with a girl who said her Uncle Thor knew everything about dragons. She tried to trap us in her barn, but we escaped. She saw our dragon and we told her we lived in Maryland near Sugarloaf Mountain. So this Thor guy knows more about our dragon. We'll warn him about that, too."

Everyone agreed that the dragon needed to know right away. They were surprised about the connection between the girl in Ohio and the professor. Annie, Nate, and Gib were sent to tell the dragon about Janey and Thor and to meet the family in the clearing on the mountain in an hour. They left the house and headed for the tree.

Sara reviewed all of her notes and asked Zoe, George, and Camille, "You are sure that this Professor Grimmstone is after the dragon?"

All three said yes and Camille explained again what the professor had said about capturing the dragon. Zoe added that if the spell the professor had found worked, the dragon would be defenseless against the chains and the cage.

Jim said, "Let's see what the dragon has to say about this. Maybe he knows more than we do and can advise us on the next steps. Let's get up to the clearing."

As soon as Annie, Gib, and Nate returned, the family hiked up Sugarloaf Mountain to the clearing. This was the trail that Sara had climbed as a child to find the dragon. The same trail that Zoe and George had climbed one stormy night. They remembered that first hike as they reached the boulder. Sara could still hear her brothers calling her a scaredy cat and daring her to go around the rock and see what was glowing a deep blue color. She had taken a deep breath and rounded the boulder to find a very sick dragon. After nursing him back to health, they had become great friends. That was many years ago and her own children had gone through a similar experience. Now here they were once again coming to save the dragon.

As the group came around the rock, Mr. Dragon flew down into the clearing. "It is so good to see all of you. Annie says that you have some bad news to share concerning a mad scientist? Tell me what you have found out."

Zoe and Camille repeated everything they had told the family while the rest waited patiently. The more the dragon heard, the more concerned he seemed to become. Finally, when the girls had finished their story, he spoke.

"Unfortunately, I know this Thor Grimmstone. Many years ago I lived on a mountain outside of New York City. This was before I met your grandmother. I befriended a family named Grimmstone and took their children on many adventures. Once when the Grimmstone children were visiting my cave and my library, one of my spell books went missing. I asked them several times where the book had gone. Two of the children swore that they had no idea. But the third one avoided my questions and after that he did not come to visit me again. I realized that I could not stay near this family if he had the spell book since I knew the book contained dangerous spells against dragons.

"Shortly after he stole the book, I packed up and moved to Sugarloaf Mountain and met your grandmother. I was so happy to be rid of the Grimmstone family I really didn't think any more about it. I decided that the boy would not know what to do with the book and it would soon be lost.

"Around the time that your mother began to visit me, I heard that a dragon had been caught and drained of his magical powers. The Dragon Council investigated and discovered that the son of the boy who stole my book had found the spell book and mistakenly used it on a dragon. The Council rescued the dragon before the boy could show the dragon off to the world, but the dragons could not find the book. Somehow the book ended up in the New York City Library where it has been safely hidden until now.

"Professor Thor is the boy who mistakenly used the spell when he was a child. He should have forgotten all about it as he grew up, so I am not sure how he has suddenly remembered. Perhaps Zoe and Camille could talk with the professor and find out why he knows so much. You would just be following up on your visit and preparing for a report that you want to write about the museum trip."

Sara looked at Jim. "I think the dragon has found a good plan to investigate this further without sneaking around or stealing anything. Zoe, do you think you and Camille can just talk to the professor and find out what he knows?"

Camille spoke first. "I think that is a brilliant plan, Mr. Dragon. The more information we have the better prepared we can be for action. Do you think we are in any danger?"

Zoe joined in. "I know we can talk to him about this. He is so excited to share what he knows and he wants to brag to anyone who will listen. Most of our classmates just laughed at him, so I am sure he will want to talk to anyone who is really interested."

Jim nodded his approval. "On one condition, girls. If he seems even a little suspicious, you say goodbye and leave. We don't know anything about this man. He might become dangerous so be wary and ready to escape." The girls agreed.

"Once we know more, we need to meet again to plan our next steps. We'll visit the museum tomorrow, so let's meet tomorrow evening around the same time."

Everyone agreed and the dragon flew off to his cave as the family made its way down the trail. "You girls are going to need a ride to the museum, so I will pick you up from school and drive you there. Then I can wait in the parking lot and make sure you are okay."

"Thanks, Dad, I think that is a good idea. Camille, will your parents be okay with this?"

"Well, you know they don't believe in the dragon, so I will just tell them I am following up on the field trip, which is the truth, and I think they will be fine with it."

Sara added, "I'll call your mom and assure her that Jim will drive you there and be waiting in the parking lot."

Sara drove Camille and Gib home while Jim and the children prepared dinner. As the family sat down to enjoy their evening meal, they held hands and George repeated the family blessing. "We are all for one and one for all. We love and protect each other. Thank you for this meal and bless us with your protection."

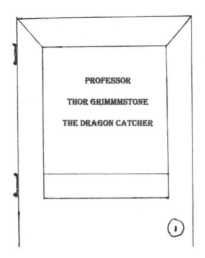

PROFESSOR

THOR GRIMMMSTONE

THE DRAGON CATCHER

Chapter 7

Interviewing Professor Grimmstone

The next day Camille and Zoe met at school. They had a long day of classes to get through before visiting the museum. They had lunch with several of their friends in the cafeteria. Camille slipped and told everyone that she and Zoe were going back to the museum to interview the professor. All the girls at the table stared at them.

"Are you guys nuts? That guy is creepy and he really believes in all this dragon nonsense."

Zoe replied, "Well, maybe there is something to all of this. Maybe there are strange things that we don't know about. It couldn't hurt to find out more."

Another girl started laughing and the rest of the table joined in the laughter. "Zoe, you have the weirdest ideas. Now I suppose you are going to tell us that you believe in dragons, right?"

"And Camille, you're her best friend so you must be a charter member of her Dragon Club, huh?"

Once the teasing got started the girls ridiculed Zoe and Camille so much that they finally got up and moved to another table. "Oh, Zoe, I am so sorry. I should have remembered to keep my mouth shut. I hope they will forget this."

"It's okay, Camille. Sometimes it isn't easy knowing things that others don't believe in. Remember when I first told you about the dragon and you told me I was crazy. It took you a while to believe. Anyways, I think they will move on to some other person to tease. They are always on the lookout for something to make a big deal out of. Let's get through the afternoon and then we can find out what this professor guy is up to."

At the end of the afternoon classes, Zoe went by her locker to get her books. A note was taped to the locker door.

'Dragon meeting tonight at the old oak tree. Be there or be square.'

Zoe took down the note and stuffed it in her pocket. Camille came along with a note from her locker, too.

"Good grief, Zoe. They won't let this go away. Look at this. 'Don't let the dragon bite you.' Can you believe this?"

"I got one, too. I'm sure they will forget by tomorrow. Let's get going."

As they walked out the front door of the school, the same group of girls were standing together waiting for their bus. "Good luck, dragon slayers! Watch out for the goofy professor! He might put the hex on you!" Then they all started to giggle.

Zoe turned to the group and waved. "Thanks for your good wishes! We'll call you if we need help!" And then Zoe and Camille got into her dad's car and drove away.

Jim asked, "What was that all about?"

"Some of the girls just want to tease us because we are going back to the museum. No biggie."

Jim shrugged his shoulders and drove the girls to the museum. As he parked the car, he told them again to leave if the professor got weird. If they didn't come out in 45 minutes he was coming in to get them. Zoe assured her dad that they were planning on a quick interview and exiting immediately. The girls went into the museum.

Camille went up to the main desk and told the receptionist that they had an appointment with Professor Grimmstone. She called him and let him know the girls had arrived. The professor came out immediately and ushered them back to his research lab and office. Although he was still pretty intense, his voice was calmer as he asked the girls what they wanted to know.

Zoe began. "I found your lecture so interesting. As a child I always thought I could see dragons and even fly on them. Some imagination, huh?"

"I am sure you were imagining that since a dragon would eat you in one gulp if you ever really did meet one. But I know dragons exist. All my research has led me to discoveries of abandoned caves outside of New York and dragon footprints in the mud around the cave. When I was a little boy, my father would tell me stories about a dragon that he would visit in a cave near his house. I know they must exist."

"I am curious about your research, professor," Camille continued. "What kind of evidence do you have that dragons still exist?"

"Ah, the best, and I think you two can understand it. My niece, Janey, lives in Ohio. She called me during the summer and told me that she not only had seen a dragon, but she had captured it in her barn. There were three trolls with the dragon and they were controlling the big lizard. The trolls said they lived on Sugarloaf Mountain with the dragon. When she trapped them in the barn, the trolls ordered the dragon to break out and the dragon burned down the barn door with his fiery breath. The dragon and the trolls escaped."

"But don't you think she might be making this up? Do you really think she saw a dragon?"

"I visited my niece the very next day and I found footprints in the mud on the barn floor. There were definitely three small trolls and a giant dragon in that barn. You could see his claw marks across the door and the door lock was melted by his breath. We were so close to catching him. And now that I know he lives on Sugarloaf Mountain, it will be easy to capture him."

"Oh my, that is exciting. The dragon sounds so violent. How can you possibly contain such a dangerous creature?" Zoe asked.

"Oh ho! I have found an ancient spell book in the New York City Public Library archives. It has a spell to take away a dragon's magic and fiery breath. Once he is disarmed it will be a simple matter of throwing some chains on him and dragging him into a cage. Then he will be mine and everyone will believe me."

Zoe and Camille were madly writing down everything the professor was telling them. "This book of spells sounds so interesting. Can we see it?"

The professor eyed the girls up and down. He thought for a moment and then said, "I guess it wouldn't hurt to show you the book. You wouldn't know what to do with it. I keep it in a safe place in my office. You wait here and I will get it."

The girls watched as the professor went into his office. They could see his reflection in the window of the office door and watched him climb on a chair and reach to the top of a cabinet. He pulled down a big white box and placed it on his desk. He opened the box and brought the dusty old book into the lab.

"Wow! That looks really old. How did you ever find it?"

"When my father died two years ago, I was going through all of his belongings, cleaning out his house. I found a letter from the library thanking him for donating the old book to their archives. There was a note from my father attached to the letter. It was addressed to me and said:

Thor

>***If you find this letter then you will know where the book is that I stole from the dragon in the cave. If you ever need it you can get it from the library. Protect yourself, son. Protect the world.***

>***Your Father***

"So, you see, my father did see a dragon when he was a boy and he did find a way to trap him with the book. My father saved the book for me. He knew I would be the one to save the world from these dangerous creatures and prove that there really are dragons."

"You know professor, we have been studying dragons in our English class and we are reading several different books about dragons. According to many of the authors adults can't see dragons. What do you think about that?"

"In my research I have discovered that some adults can see dragons if they truly believe in them. Since I have devoted my life's work to dragons, I believe in them and I know I will be able to see him."

"But, if you put him in a cage for others to see, why will they believe and how will they be able to see him? Do you think your father would approve of this?" asked Camille.

The professor stopped and stared at Camille. "Young lady, I think you are asking too many negative questions. You need to focus on my great work and how I will rid the world of these evil reptiles. You need to write a report about what a great scientist I am and how I will capture and destroy dragons."

"I am sure that Camille didn't mean anything disrespectful, sir. But I did want to ask you about the idea that all dragons are evil. Many books portray them as friendly and sometimes they are even heroes saving people. Do you think those books are inaccurate?"

"You two seem to know a lot about dragons, but you have wrong information. You need to read more carefully and study my research. Those books that portray dragons as good and kind are all fiction. I believe they may even have been written by dragons and trolls to try and trick us into trusting them. I have read the ancient texts that prove that they are all evil and they must be destroyed to protect mankind from extinction. I must find the dragon and these trolls and destroy them. They will be the first in my quest to rid the world of dragons!"

The professor's voice was beginning to rise and his eyes were beginning to get that crazy look that he had during the lecture with the school group. Zoe gave Camille the signal and Camille ended the interview.

"Thank you so very much for sharing your time and your brilliant research with us, professor. I think you are going to save the world and we can write a really positive and thorough article about this now."

The girls stood up and shook the professor's hand and left his office before he could say any more. They were in the car with Jim within minutes.

"Let's get out of here. That guy really is crazy and we don't want him following us home or anything."

"What happened in there?"

"We'll tell you, just start driving."

Jim started the car and left the parking lot as the professor came out of the front door. He watched them drive away as Zoe told her dad everything that had happened in the lab.

Chapter 8

Family Updates

While Zoe and Camille were at the museum, George was dealing with his own problems. He was co-captain of the school's soccer team with Gregory Simson. After practice, Gregory came up to George in the locker room and poked his finger in George's chest.

"Listen here, George. In the next game, I am going to score all of the goals. You better stay out of my way and pass me the ball or else. You got it?"

George was surprised by Gregory's behavior. "Well, Greg, we play on a team. If you are in a position to score I am certainly going to pass the ball to you because I want the team to win. But if someone else can get the goal, then I will pass it to him. We want the team to win."

"You aren't listening to me, buddy. I get the ball and I score the goals and I am the hero or else."

George raised his voice and stared at Gregory. "Or else what?"

Gregory puffed out his chest and poked George again. "Or else you are going to get seriously hurt out there on the field."

George grabbed Gregory's wrist and twisted his hand until Gregory screamed and fell to the ground. "Team, Gregory. And don't ever poke me like that again or you won't be playing in any game for a long time." George walked away leaving Gregory on the floor crying.

Now he felt terrible. He had hurt someone and he had threatened him. That wasn't anything like the way he behaved. He had never done anything like that before. He couldn't decide if he had to apologize to Gregory or what to do. As he rode the bus home, he couldn't sort things out. He must see the dragon and get some advice. He arrived in the kitchen just as Zoe and Jim drove into the driveway after dropping Camille at her house.

Sara looked at George and could tell something was wrong. "George, are you okay? What's wrong?"

"It's nothing, Mom. I can handle it. But I think I want to see the dragon this afternoon."

Zoe and Jim came into the kitchen and told George and Sara that they needed to talk about the dragon situation. The four settled down at the kitchen table and Zoe outlined everything that the professor had said.

"I really think this guy knows something about a spell and I think he is dangerous. His information is too accurate. He really has found out about the real world of dragons even if he also believes a lot of the myths. If he finds out about our fairy powers it will get even worse. What should we do?"

Sara said, "It's time to get the dragon's advice. He must know what to do about all of this. I'll send Annie and Nate to get him." Sara left the kitchen to find the twins and send them on their way. Jim went out to the car to get his briefcase from work. Zoe looked at George. She could hear him thinking about soccer.

"Hey, are you okay? Why is soccer bothering you? I can hear your thoughts, George. What's up?"

"Oh, it's just this kid at school. I guess I want you to know about it, so that is why I am sending you telepathic messages. Gregory is the other captain of our soccer team. After practice today he started pushing me around in the locker room and telling me to pass the ball to him so he could score all the goals and be a hero. I kept telling him we were a team and I would pass the ball to whoever had the best chance of scoring. He pushed me again, so I grabbed his hand and forced him to the ground. I threatened to really hurt him if he didn't leave me alone. I feel so badly, Zoe. I never hurt people or threaten them. I need to talk with the dragon about this."

Zoe patted his shoulder. "We'll figure this out, George. The dragon will know what to do. Let's get ready for the meeting."

The clearing on the mountain was the safest place for the family and the dragon to gather, so they all climbed the mountain for the meeting. The dragon listened thoughtfully to everything that Zoe described. Then he explained what he knew.

"This is what I feared. Thor Grimmstone's father is indeed the same person who stole one of my spell books many years ago. The book does contain spells that will take away a dragon's powers. And even though Thor is an adult, his strong belief in dragons will enable him to see me. But the problem goes deeper.

"The spell that he is planning to use is a black cloud that spreads across the land like fog and disables all magical creatures. Depending on how much he creates, it could affect creatures for miles around, including your fairy powers." The dragon pointed at the four children.

"Is there any way to stop it?" Zoe asked.

"The best way is to prevent it from even being made or released. Once he releases the fog into the air I am not sure what can be done. The Leaf Fairy will know. We must visit her first thing tomorrow to find out if there is any possible way to counteract the spell."

The dragon turned to Sara and Jim. "I am sorry to put your family in this dangerous position. We must find a way to get the spell book and destroy whatever he has made. This spell will be a danger to many and not just me. Unfortunately I do not know what it will do to the children since they are a unique blend of magical fairies and humans. We must protect them from the fog."

There was a lengthy discussion of how to stop the professor, get the book, and destroy the spell. The group decided to think about all of this overnight and then the children would visit the Leaf Fairy in the Enchanted Forest in the morning. Using whatever information she could provide, the group would meet again and plan. As the family prepared to hike down the mountain, George told his dad that he wanted to talk with the dragon alone, so he would be along shortly. The rest of the family left and George sat down with the dragon.

"Well George, how are things going? Enjoying middle school?"

"Yes, I am. There are a lot of wonderful things happening in my life and I have a lot of good friends. We are learning many new ideas in school and I especially enjoy the history classes. My soccer team is doing great, but that is what I want to talk about."

The dragon leaned against a rock and put one of his claws to his lips. "What's going on, George?"

"Gregory is the co-captain of the team with me. Our coach tells us all the time that we are a team and we need to pass the ball and win as a team. I think that is what has made us so successful. Many of the guys score goals and we have won every game this season. So today, Gregory corners me in the locker room and starts pushing on me. He tells me to pass the ball to him so he can score all the goals and win the games. He wants to be a big soccer hero."

The dragon raised his eyebrows. "So what did you do?"

"I tried to talk to him and explain about team work and everybody scoring. I told him I would pass the ball to whichever teammate had the best shot. We would play as a team."

"And?"

"And he shoved me again and told me to pass the ball to him or else. I tried to tell him again about the team, but he put his finger on my chest and threatened me. So I grabbed his hand and forced him to the ground and told him to never touch me again or he would be sorry. Then I walked away."

"And now you feel terrible that you hurt someone and threatened them."

"Yeah, how did you know that?"

"George, it is really important to try and talk things out. It is really important to avoid physical violence and verbal threats. Most of the time problems can be solved by talking it out. But sometimes others will push you too far and you must defend yourself. Gregory pushed too far. First you need to try to talk with Gregory and see if you can patch things up. Hopefully Gregory was just having a bad day and everything will be all right.

"But if he continues to threaten you, then you need to talk with your coach. Tell him you are not trying to be a tattletale and you want his advice on what you should do.

Tell the coach that you would like to be able to solve this on your own. What would he suggest? I think he will give you good advice."

"Thanks, Mr. Dragon. I can always count on you to listen and make some helpful suggestions. We'll see you in the morning ready to visit the Enchanted Forest."

George waved goodbye and started down the trail. Halfway down the mountain he met Zoe. "I was coming back up to check on you. Everything okay?"

"Yes, the dragon had good ideas, so I think it will work out. Let's get some sleep so we are ready for tomorrow morning. Good thing we don't have school tomorrow."

Hand in hand, brother and sister went down the trail with many thoughts swirling in their heads.

Chapter 9

<u>The Engine Castle</u>

It was a beautiful sunrise over the mountain the next day. Zoe, George, Nate, and Annie were all dressed and ready to go. They had a wonderful breakfast with their parents enjoying the yummy pancakes and syrup and big glasses of orange juice. Gib and Camille arrived shortly after nine and then the six children set out to climb the trail to the clearing on the mountain. As they hiked they talked about the dragon and different adventures they had enjoyed with him.

When they reached the clearing the dragon was waiting for them. He had brought six backpacks with water and lots of peanut butter and jelly sandwiches. The children were really pleased, especially Zoe, George, and Camille. It had been a long time since they had been on an adventure with the dragon and they were looking forward to riding on his back once more.

The six climbed aboard and the dragon flew up into the clouds. In no time they descended into the Enchanted Forest. Zoe remembered how beautiful the forest could be, and also how dangerous. The group found the glowing pink pathway to the Leaf Fairy's tree and ran all the way to the edge of her clearing. The dragon announced their arrival with a gentle roar and the fairy came out to greet them.

"I knew you would be back. I just wasn't sure how long it would take for you to figure things out. I see you have brought more children. I don't think they are all fairies though."

"Leaf, you are so observant. You know Annie and Nate. This is Zoe and George, the sister and brother who were turned into fairies. These two are their friends, Camille and Gib. We've come for some information."

"Of course you have, Dragon. Come, let's have a seat and enjoy some fairy snacks while we talk." Leaf flitted away to her tree and the group followed her. When they reached the bottom of the oak, they found a large bench and a table.

"Please have a seat and I'll get some of the honey cakes." Leaf returned with a large plate of her famous honey cakes and a pitcher of water. She waved her hand and plates, napkins, cups, and forks flew out of the tree and onto the table. The children were enjoying her presentation.

"Pardon me, Miss Fairy, but could we have some of your honey tea? It was so delicious last time." Annie was a big fan of tea and she thought the honey tea was especially good.

Leaf beamed a big smile at the dragon. "Of course, Annie. I'll be right back." Leaf zoomed into the tree and came back with a bright yellow pot of tea. She poured tea into everyone's cups except for the dragon. They all enjoyed their cakes and tea.

"Let's save a little time here. Zoe, you and Camille must lean your heads here so I can touch them. Then all the information about this crazy professor will just float into my head. Okay?"

Camille looked at the fairy. "Well, are you going to collect all my thoughts or just the ones about the professor?"

Leaf giggled her little fairy laugh. "Oh dear, Camille. I won't touch your thoughts about your new boyfriend or any of that other stuff. I just need the information about the professor." Camille blushed and Gib started laughing.

Zoe and Camille leaned forward and put their heads together with Leaf. In a few moments Leaf flew backwards. "Oh my, we do have a problem here. We can deal with the professor easily, but the spell itself is much more dangerous. You must always be careful around the black fog. Don't let it touch you or you will lose all your fairy powers. That means if you are flying, you will fall. Be very careful.

"The spell must be forced back into its original space and then it will explode and destroy itself. Here is how you will do this." Leaf gave the children detailed instructions on how to force the cloud of fog back into its original vessel.

"And now I must ask you for a favor in return. A dear sweet princess has been captured and locked up in the Engine Castle. This castle is like a giant machine run by robots. I cannot use my magic on machines like the castle, so I cannot free her. I need you to go to the castle and free the princess." The dragon sat back in the shadows while the children eagerly questioned Leaf.

"Where is this castle?"

"You will return to the large clearing and take the glowing blue pathway. When you reach the end you will see the castle across a meadow. The castle is guarded by robots and they are very strong. Once they grab you, you cannot escape their grasp."

"Do you know if they have any weaknesses? Is there any way into the castle other than the front gate?"

"You have trained them well, Dragon. They know what to ask and I can see their planning wheels are already turning in their heads. The only way into the castle is through the front gate and the rest of the castle has very high stone walls. Much of what goes on there is secret, but I do know that everything runs on electricity."

George spoke up. "That's the way we'll do it. We need to short out the electricity. Then the whole castle will stop working." Zoe and Camille remembered from their science classes about shorting out electricity. The younger ones had no idea what they were talking about.

Zoe turned to the little ones. "Annie, Gib, and Nate. You need to stay here with Mr. Dragon and Leaf."

"But we want to go. We want to fight the robots. We want to save the princess, too!"

Zoe chose her words carefully. "You will be a very important part of the mission. This will be the home base and you must protect it from any robots that might escape or chase after us. When we bring the princess back you must keep her safe and check her out to be sure she is all right. Can you do that?"

The three nodded their heads vigorously. "We'll be ready, Zoe. Go get the princess!"

The dragon smiled and winked at Zoe. Camille, George, and Zoe ran down the pink pathway back to the main clearing.

"Man, Zoe, that was some fast thinking with the little ones. You sounded so convincing." Camille patted Zoe on the back.

"Good job, sis!"

When the three reached the main clearing, they found the glowing blue pathway. It did not take long to reach the meadow. They knelt down in the weeds and looked over the situation. George pointed at the guards at the main gate.

Camille pointed across the meadow to a nearby lake. Zoe pointed at their three heads and pulled them together. As long as their heads were touching, Camille could talk through her thoughts with Zoe and George.

Camille thought, "Put water on the robots and that should cause everything to short out. The whole castle should stop working."

George thought, "But how do we get enough water over onto the guards?"

The three looked around the edge of the meadow. Zoe pointed to a cluster of bamboo plants. She thought, "Look, there are several on the ground. They are hollow. We could suck some water up into the bamboo like straws and then squirt it at the robots."

George returned the thought, "That's a good idea, but I am not sure that we have enough strength to suck water into the shoots and then carry them to the robots. But we could fly the water over the robots and the castle and drop it on them. Is there anything we can use to carry the water?"

Zoe pointed to the backpacks. "They are waterproof to keep the water out in a rain storm which means they will also keep water in. It works both ways."

"Now you're thinking," Camille thought. "Let's crawl over to the lake. I can fill up the bags and you two can fly them over the castle. How many bags of water do you think it will take, George?"

"I think we need to concentrate the water in one place to flood the machinery. I'm going to fly up really high and see if I can spot anything." George flew straight up in the air as fast as he could. Zoe and Camille watched him zoom high over the castle. He was back in just a moment.

George whispered, "I see the main electricity source. There is a generator in the middle of the castle. If we can pour enough water into that, it will short out and explode."

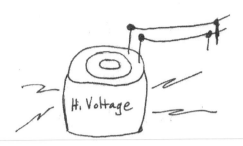

"Then let's do it." The three crawled through the meadow grass to the lake. Camille filled all three of the backpacks. She could have one ready each time Zoe or George returned.

"Ready, George?" George nodded and the two took off for the castle carrying their backpacks full of water.

At first the guards did not see them. They were able to fly into the middle of the castle and dump the first two backpacks of water right into the generator and fly back out to the lake. The guards saw them on the return flight.

Camille handed the next bag to George and he took off. Then she filled Zoe's bag and she followed. The guards saw Camille and began to move across the meadow towards her. Zoe and George were able to make three trips before the guards got close to Camille. On their return trip they swooped down and grabbed Camille by her arms and flew her up over the guards. The robots made all kinds of noises trying to reach the children and grab them.

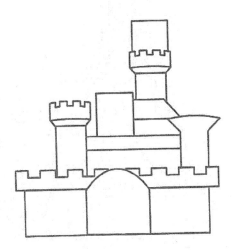

The three flew across the meadow to the entrance to the castle. "Let's get in there and see where the princess is." And then they heard the terrible crackling sounds and they saw the generator shooting sparks and it was turning red and orange with too much heat and then----KABOOM!. The blast knocked the children off their feet and they fell outside the gate. George was up first and grabbed Zoe and then Camille and they went inside.

"It worked! The generator is broken down. Look at all the robots. Every one of them has stopped working. We did it."

"Now where is the princess?" They looked everywhere and finally heard a tiny voice shouting from above. "Oh dear, oh dear. I am trapped up in this tower and I cannot get down."

Zoe pointed up to the window. "Let's go, George."

The two flew up to the tower window and grabbed the princess. They flew her safely to the ground and then told her they were there to save her. She said, "Thank you for coming, but we must move fast. The giant who built this castle will return to fix it very soon. Where do we go?"

Camille pointed the way and they ran for the main gate. The ground began to shake and they could tell that the giant was coming. They saw him at the edge of the meadow. He saw them at the gate. In a loud and raging voice he bellowed, "You cannot take my princess. She is mine. I will destroy all of you!"

As the giant began to run towards the castle, Zoe looked at George. "We must use all of our power to fly these two to safety. Are you ready?" She turned to Camille. "Climb onto my back and hold on tight. You, Princess, get on George's back." Both girls did as they were told and just as the giant was reaching the gate, the four flew straight up into the clouds. He shook his fists at them and screamed some horrible sound and then they were in the clouds.

After a few minutes, Zoe pointed to the main clearing. They landed in the clearing and Camille and the princess climbed off of their backs. The four stood smiling at each other. "Can you believe that? I didn't know you could carry me on your back! We're going to have to do that more often!"

George and Zoe were smiling and breathing heavily. "They were pretty heavy, huh?"

"Yeah, you would think a little princess wouldn't weigh so much."

"Hey, are you calling me fat?" The princess poked George in the ribs.

George blushed and was flustered. "No, your highness. I mean you are very skinny. Or no, you are just thin. I mean you look really nice and normal. No, I mean you're beautiful. I mean…."

"George was just saying that carrying anyone on our backs is a little tough. Right, Camille?" George's face was turning beet red and he was looking at the ground.

Camille grinned. "Yeah, partner. Those flying fairy powers are built for just one person so you really had to work at it."

"So you ARE fairies. Funny, you don't look like fairies. All the fairies I know have pointy ears and wings and they are much smaller than you. And…"

"Slow down, Princess. The Leaf Fairy sent us to rescue you and she is waiting for you down the pink path. Let's not keep her waiting."

Zoe pointed towards the path. Camille led the way, then the princess, followed by George and Zoe. He grinned sheepishly at Zoe and she put her arm around his shoulder. "It's okay little brother, she's just a girl."

They reached the fairy's tree and the princess and the Leaf Fairy were so happy to see each other. The dragon and the children said their goodbyes and flew out of the Enchanted Forest back to Sugarloaf Mountain.

"That was quite the adventure, Mr. Dragon. At least the Leaf Fairy could tell us what to do if Professor Thor releases the spell. You heard her say that you must stay in your cave and seal it up so the fog doesn't get in, right?"

"Yes, Zoe, I heard her warning. But I do not intend to let you all get hurt at my expense. I will do whatever I have to do to protect all of you."

"We'll talk about this again. We need to find out how soon the professor is planning to use his spell."

Chapter 10

A Revealing Tale

After a good night's sleep, Zoe met with her three siblings in the big window in the twins' room. The four enjoyed watching the sun rise over the mountain especially in the fall when the leaves began to change color. "Oooo, look at the trees glowing in the sunlight. Soon their leaves will turn that golden yellow color and the mountain will look like a pile of gold."

"In a few more weeks, Annie. I can wait for fall to officially start since that means that winter is close behind and I am not looking forward to all that snow again this year."

"Oh, George, you just don't like having to shovel the driveway," Annie teased.

"You got that right. But I think that you and Nate are getting old enough now that you can help." He smiled and Annie and Nate frowned.

"All right, you guys. We need to focus on the present, not weeks from now. Let's outline all the steps." Zoe took out a big sheet of paper and began to make a list of everything the fairy had told them. The other three helped her remember every detail. When she was finished they had a pretty clear map of the operation.

"Step one will have to wait until tomorrow when Camille and I will return to the professor's lab and try to find out more about his research and when he is planning to act. Then we'll know what to do from there. Camille and I are headed to the mall this afternoon to buy some supplies for the operation. George is headed to soccer practice. And I would assume that you guys are headed for the dragon's cave?"

"You bet. We asked him if we could just rest in his library and read books all day. Those books are so cool the way they act out the story with little figures floating over the book. You really don't even have to read."

"Which is a good thing for two kindergartners who are just learning how to read," George pointed out.

"Let's get down to breakfast and then everybody will have a good day."

The four got dressed and headed down to a scrumptious Sunday breakfast. Sara and Jim had worked together to make omelets, fresh blueberry muffins, a big bowl of fresh fruit, and glasses of orange juice. The family dug in and enjoyed a wonderful meal together.

They talked about the weather and the changing seasons. Jim listed several chores they needed to do before winter. Sara reminded everyone that they would be going to the local apple orchard next weekend to collect apples for making applesauce and cider. George pointed out that he had a soccer game next Saturday, too. And Zoe made the surprise announcement that she and Camille were going to the school dance next Saturday night. The twins sat quietly listening to all the family news. Finally, they were able to say something.

"We're going to visit the dragon."

"Okay, you two. Have fun and tell us all about your adventure tonight at dinner."

Everyone carried their dishes to the sink and then set out on their various projects for the day. Jim drove Zoe over to Camille's house, picked up Gib, and then dropped George off at his soccer practice. Sara cleaned up the kitchen and then went about cleaning the house. When Gib arrived, the Three Caballeros headed for the big oak tree and knocked three times. They were on their way.

When they arrived at the dragon's cave, they talked some about the professor. The twins and Gib really didn't understand all the details, but the twins knew they would have to use their magical powers at some point. Then they settled down in the dragon's library with some good storybooks. Nate chose a story about knights and kings and castles. He liked the shiny armor and the big horses. Gib grabbed a book about cars and trucks and how they worked. He was so clever and could figure out any machine. Annie chose a story about a dragon family that was going shopping at the Dragon Mall. Soon they were deep into their stories.

Annie reached a point in the story where there was a magic spell. Without even thinking she repeated the spell out loud and suddenly there was a huge whoosh of wind and she found Nate, Gib, and herself inside the book. Somehow they had joined the story and they were now characters in the dragon's family. They even looked like dragons!

The mother dragon came over to the table in the story and said, "Well, it is about time you three made it to breakfast. We have yummy toads and lizards to go along with your fried turtle eggs. Eat up, you have a busy day of shopping ahead."

Annie, Nate, and Gib looked at each other. They began to laugh. "You look so funny in that dragon costume, Annie."

"Green looks good on you, too, Gib. And Nate, you have such big red eyes."

The three were surprised to find that they enjoyed the lizards and toads and the fried turtle eggs. In their minds they thought "yuck" but in their mouths it was delicious. The mother dragon said, "You must hurry up now, your father is taking you to the mall."

Then Mr. Dragon walked into the kitchen. Annie was positive that this was their dragon, but she addressed the dragon as Father. She couldn't believe the words coming out of her dragon mouth. Nate and Gib looked at her and then said, "Good morning, Father," to the dragon. It seemed like the children could read each other's minds in this story. They were talking back and forth in their heads but then speaking like dragon children in the story.

"Nate, why are we calling him Father? Do you think the dragon really has children?"

"I don't know, Gib, but it seems like we are supposed to be his children in this story. This is really weird."

"Look, you two, this is a story and we just have to play along until we can figure out how to get out of the story. We're trapped here right now!"

In the story the three dragon children replied that they were ready to go to the mall. Mr. Dragon took them out to his bright green minivan and they all piled inside, buckling their seatbelts for the trip. The dragon raced down the highway and soon they saw a huge mall full of all kinds of stores. The dragon parked the minivan and they went inside.

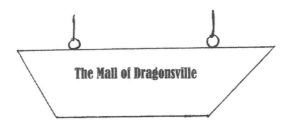

As they walked along, Annie saw many familiar stores, except the names were different. There was a restaurant called McDragon where you could get hamburgers and fries. There was a clothing store called JC Dragons and all the clothes in the windows were designed for dragons. There was a shoe store called the Dragon Shoe Warehouse and the shoes were beautiful, shaped for the dragons' claws.

Nate saw a sports store called Dragon Authority and a pizza place called Pizza Cave. There were hundreds of dragons roaming the mall carrying shopping bags and talking to each other. Then Mr. Dragon told them to come with him. They went into the biggest toy store they had ever seen, Dragon Toy Heaven.

"You may each choose one toy to take home today."

Even though they knew they were children and not dragons, Annie, Gib, and Nate were excited and ran through the store choosing their favorite toys. They came to the counter to purchase their toys, but Mr. Dragon was gone. They looked across the mall and saw three knights dragging him away in chains. They did not understand what was happening until more knights grabbed them and put them in chains. They dragged them out of the mall and shoved them into a cage on a truck. Their father was in another cage on a different truck.

The trucks drove away from the mall. They could see a large black castle coming into view. As they passed through the castle gate, they suddenly felt a tremendous burst of wind and Annie, Nate, and Gib found themselves sitting in the dragon's cave on his couch. Mr. Dragon was standing over them.

"My goodness, children. How did you get inside that storybook? I'm glad I realized where you were so I could pull you out in time. What did you see?"

All three jumped up and hugged the dragon. Annie explained how she had said the spell and they were sucked into the story. She told the dragon what they saw in the story. They didn't understand why Mr. Dragon had a family. They had so many questions.

The dragon asked them to sit down on the couch. "I thought this was just another one of the tales that I have on my library shelves. Now that you describe what happened, I am beginning to remember." The dragon tapped his head.

"Many years ago I think I did have a family and we lived happily in a place called Dragonsville. My wife and I had a comfortable cave and we raised our three children there. I remember one morning I took my children to the mall for some shopping. We were in a toy store and many of the king's knights ran into the store and tied me up in chains. Then they captured my children. We were all put in cages on trucks. I saw my children leave the mall in one truck that drove in the opposite direction from me. I learned later that my wife was also in that cage. My whole family was taken from me and I didn't know where they went.

"The knights took me to a high cliff above the Dark Blue Sea. They tied me in many chains and told me that I had threatened the king and I would pay with my life. They pushed me off of the cliff and I fell a thousand feet into the Dark Blue Sea. I could not free myself from the chains and I could not swim. The last thing I remembered was the dark blue water all around me and wishing that I could save my family."

Nate, Annie, and Gib all stared at the dragon. "You mean the story was real? You have a family?"

"I HAD a family. I woke up on a beach somewhere that I had never been. There were two fishermen who were taking the chains off of me. One said, 'This poor dragon. How could anyone do this to such a beautiful animal?'

When I was free I sat up and spread my wings. The man said, 'You are free now. Go do some good in this world.' He turned and walked away."

"Is that why you are here in our world?"

"Somehow I had traveled through the Dark Blue Sea to this world. I searched everywhere for my family, but I could never find them. Then one day I accidentally landed in a cave and discovered many other dragons. They were all friendly and welcomed me. One stepped forward and said he was the Master Dragon. I spent a long time with him learning about why we were here in your world. All the dragons had lost their families the same way."

"We saw you captured in the mall. We saw them drag you away. We were your children in the book. We know where they took your family."

The dragon raised his head and stared into their eyes. "Yes, I can see that you have lived the story. We were all the father dragons and we were banished from the kingdom and thrown into the Dark Blue Sea. Eventually all the father dragons came here. But we never knew what happened to our families. You have seen where our children have been taken?"

"Yes, we were locked in a big cage on the back of a truck and we went to a huge black castle. We were going through the gate when you grabbed us out of the story."

Mr. Dragon sat down in his rocking chair. "It is as I feared. The wicked king did kidnap all our families. I must tell the other father dragons what you have found out. Thank you, children for your bravery. You need to go home now and I will see you again soon." The dragon took the storybook and put it up on his fireplace mantle. The children said goodbye and headed down the yellow pathway.

"Annie, I don't understand all of this," Gib said.

"I don't either, Gib. But we will tell my mom and she will know what to do. Let's go."

The three ran down the path and up the stairs. They burst through the doorway in the tree and raced to the house. They found Sara sitting at the kitchen table waiting for their report of the day's adventures.

"You won't believe what we just found out."

Chapter 11

<u>The Forbidden Mountain</u>

On Monday afternoon right after school, Jim drove Zoe and Camille to the museum. He knew they had to find out what the professor was up to, but he was not comfortable with them going in there again. "Zoe, you have your mom's cellphone. All you have to do is push the emergency button and I will be in there in seconds. Be careful with this man. I think he may be crazy."

"I agree, Dad. We'll be careful and the moment we feel in danger, you'll know."

The girls entered the museum and once again told the receptionist they were there to interview Professor Grimmstone. Within a few minutes the professor came out and greeted the girls.

"So, you two have come back to learn more about my research? I knew you couldn't resist."

Zoe and Camille gave the professor big smiles. "We were so fascinated as we wrote our report that we just had to come back and learn more about your brilliant theory. Can we ask you a few more questions?"

"But of course. Come this way." The professor led them down a hallway towards his research lab. Suddenly the lights went out and it was pitch black. Zoe and Camille grabbed hands and moved to the wall. There was a strange wailing sound and a whirling gush of warm air. The girls felt like they were flying and then they bumped into a solid wall. Zoe whispered to Camille, "Stay calm and let's get down low. We must be sure that we continue to hold hands so we don't get separated. I'm getting out my flashlight."

"Is it time to call your dad?"

"I don't think so. I'm not sure he could even find us in this dark place. Let's see if we can find out what is going on." Zoe turned on her flashlight and covered the lens so that only a little bit of light shone through her fingers. She slowly guided the light around them. They saw stone walls and a wooden door. Then they saw flashes of light under the door.

"Something is going on beyond that door. Let's find out what."

Together the girls crawled to the door. Zoe turned off her flashlight and put it away. "Ready?"

"You bet I'm ready. Let's see what this guy is up to."

Camille slowly opened the door just a crack to see what was going on. The girls could not believe what they were seeing. In the middle of the room there was just one table with a large crystal ball on it. The crystal ball kept flashing a bright light. They cautiously went into the room and walked over to the table.

"Zoe, it's a crystal ball. You can see into the future with this. Do you know how to make it work?"

"Never seen one but my fairy intuition tells me to just talk to it and command it to tell me what I want to know. Here goes."

"Crystal ball, tell me where I am."

A really creepy voice echoed from the glowing crystal. It sounded just like a witch in one of those horror movies. "You are on the Forbidden Mountain. This is the powerful lab of the evil sorcerer Thor. He was summoned here today because his spell is ready and you were brought because you were with him."

"Show me where to find the professor and his magic potion."

The crystal ball glowed and then the girls could see the lab inside the crystal. "There are two doors in this room. You must take the left door to reach the lab. You will find the professor there preparing his potion." They watched the professor at work. They saw a large bowl that was steaming and bubbling.

"When will the professor use the potion?"

The crystal glowed once more and Zoe and Camille could see a black cloud of fog spreading across the farmland. "The professor has announced to the spirits of the mountain that he will use the spell at five o'clock right before sundown."

"Zoe, it's already four o'clock. It's going to happen really soon!"

"Tell me how to get off the Forbidden Mountain."

The crystal was silent. "I command you to tell me how to get off this mountain."

"I cannot tell you since you are a prisoner here. I can tell you that you should not go through the right door. There is great danger behind that doorway."

"Are there any other openings in this room?"

The crystal glowed again. "There is a window behind the red curtain, clever girl." Then the crystal went silent and stopped glowing. The room was once again pitch black and Zoe pulled out her flashlight.

"Let's find that curtain." With the bright flashlight the girls quickly found the red curtain. Camille grabbed the middle of the curtain and pulled it open. A large open window looked out over the Maryland countryside.

"Zoe, over there, that's Sugarloaf Mountain. And there is the town and the museum." Camille was pointing as she spoke.

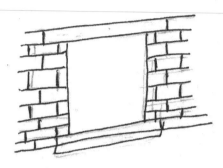

"Good thing we learned that you could fly on my back. I think it is time for us to go. We've got to hurry and warn everyone."

Camille climbed on Zoe's back and the girls flew out of the window and down to the museum parking lot. They landed behind some trees and then ran to the car. They jumped in.

"Get to the house, Dad. It's all going to happen at five o'clock."

Jim raced across town and arrived at the farmhouse at 4:15. He had called ahead and told everyone to meet on the front porch.

Chapter 12

The Black Fog

Annie, Nate, Gib, George, and Sara were waiting on the front porch. Jim and the girls ran to the house. George said, "I have already told the twins to stay with us. Gib knows that he will go with Camille to the cave and stay with the dragon. Mom and Dad will stay in the house. Anything else?"

"That's it, George." Zoe turned to Camille and Gib. "It is really important that you keep the dragon inside his cave and keep all the doors and windows closed. He will want to leave and come out to help us. Keep telling him that he will help us by staying away from the fog. If we fail to stop the fog I am not sure what will happen. If we can't contain the fog, it will take our powers away and it will seek out the dragon. Then we'll have to deal with the professor just as people with no special powers. Is everyone clear about your jobs? Are we ready?"

Everyone nodded and then George said, "Our family blessing." They held hands in a circle and repeated, "We are all for one and one for all. We love and protect each other. Bless us with your protection." Then Gib took Camille to the tree and helped her squeeze through the little opening. He led her down the staircase and up the yellow path to the dragon's cave. They greeted the dragon and got him busy playing a board game.

Sara and Jim went into the house and closed all the shutters and the front door. They sat in one of the front windows and watched their children through a small opening in the shutter. Jim said, "They certainly are brave little people. I think we have done okay with them."

"I think we have done a great job! They are confident and smart and they are kind. You couldn't ask for a better blend of strength and compassion. I just hope they can pull this off. Jim, do you know what the Leaf Fairy told them?"

"Zoe would not share it with me. She said we had to trust they knew what to do."

Jim and Sara saw their four children stand in a line in front of the house. Then they saw the cloud. It was a terrifying mass of black fog swirling and creeping across the land. There was lightning inside the cloud. It looked like pure evil and Sara was very worried for her children.

Zoe, George, Annie, and Nate stood shoulder to shoulder with their white farmhouse behind them and the mountain behind the house. They faced the swirling black cloud headed right for them. The wind was getting stronger and the noise was deafening. The lightning was becoming more intense as the fog rolled across the land.

The noise was so loud, Zoe used her telepathy to speak with her siblings. "Are we ready for this?"

The twins responded through their thoughts, "Yeah! Let's do it!"

George thought, "On my count, we begin Operation Save the Dragon!" The children raised their hands and waited.

"Ready! One....Two....Three...."

All four children pointed their hands at the giant cloud and they began to move their hands in a circular motion, always clockwise. The fog began to swirl in the same direction as their hand motions, but it kept coming at them.

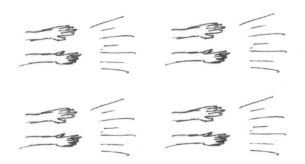

Then Zoe shouted above the roaring winds and thought at the same time, "Now!"

The four flew into the air and they began to fly at the fog. As they swirled their hands around and around, they chanted, "Back to your vessel, back to your vessel." They also began to move their hands back and forth, pushing the fog away.

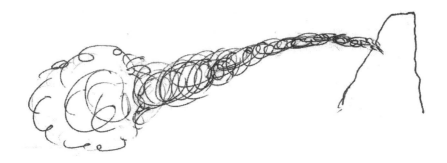

The fog acted like an animal moving from side to side trying to get around the children. But it cowered back through the valley towards the Forbidden Mountain. The spell was working and the fog was retreating. The children continued to fly at the fog pushing it back with their swirling hands. The fog was now above the mountain spinning like a funnel cloud. The mountain was shaking and the children continued their work.

Suddenly the funnel cloud was sucked into the mountain and then there was a loud explosion and one side of the mountain collapsed into itself. The ground shook and there was big plume of dust and debris as the side of the mountain caved in. The fog was gone.

"Let's go." Zoe led the others back to the farmhouse and they landed in front of the house.

Jim and Sara ran out to see them. "Are you all right?" They hugged the children and checked each one for any injuries. The twins were fine, but George and Zoe both had burns on their hands. "Oh my goodness, how did that happen?"

"We were pushing really hard on that fog and I think a little bit of it got on our hands. They hurt a lot. Can you get something for burns?"

They took the children inside and Zoe and George sat at the kitchen table. Jim brought soap and water and began to wash the burns. The water stung, but they could see black liquid oozing out of the wounds and dripping into the bowl. When the water ran clear, Jim knew he had removed the poison. Then Sara put a special ointment on the burns made from aloe. "This will heal the burns quickly." She wrapped their hands in clean cloth.

The children were relieved that the fog was gone, but they were worried about how the dragon was doing. Annie and Nate went to the tree to find out. When they arrived at the dragon's doorway, the door was shut and locked. They pounded on the door. "Camille? Gib? Mr. Dragon? Are you in there?"

Annie could hear Gib shouting through the thick door. "Is it safe, Annie?"

"Yes! We destroyed the fog. Open up."

They heard several locks clicking and finally the door swung open. They rushed inside. Camille was sitting on the couch with the dragon. Annie and Nate ran up to the dragon. "We did it! We did it, Mr. Dragon! We stopped the fog. You are safe!"

The dragon looked up and smiled. "Thank you, children. You have done a great thing today. Are George and Zoe okay?"

"They got burned a little, but Mom and Dad are fixing them up. It's over, Mr. Dragon. We won."

"Let's go check on Zoe and George." Camille unlocked the door on the cave entrance and the four children climbed aboard the dragon's back and flew out into the bright blue sky. It felt so good to be in the clear cool air. They drifted down to the farmhouse and met with Zoe, George, Jim, and Sara in the backyard. Everyone was greatly relieved and very happy.

Chapter 13

Until I Forget

      Professor Grimmstone was sitting in his research lab at the museum trying to piece together what had happened. He had the spell book in his hands and he thought he had released the black fog. Wasn't he in the secret lab on the mountain when he did that? How did he end up back here at the museum?

      Memories began to clear in his head. He had been talking to those two girls and then he was suddenly whooshed away to the secret mountain lab. That meant the potion was ready. He had opened the spell book and he started the chant. Then the potion had started to bubble and turn into a black fog. As it grew it had left the lab through the open window. It just grew and grew until the whole sky had turned black.

He remembered that he could see Sugarloaf Mountain in the distance. The black fog was headed right for it. He was going to catch his dragon. Then suddenly the fog seemed to start swirling around like a funnel cloud. And then it started coming back into the lab and flowing back into the bowl on the lab table. He saw four images flying through the sky, pointing at the fog. Were those people? Were they those trolls? Who were those forms?

The black fog had kept pouring back into the lab and everything was starting to vibrate and shake. He knew the lab was going to burst so he grabbed the spell book and ran for the door. The last thing he could remember was a bright flash and loud boom. And then he was sitting here in the museum. Everything had been going according to plan until those four beings appeared. He would find out who they were and then he would make the potion again and this time he would get the dragon even if he had to shoot those flying forms out of the sky to do it.

* * * * * * * *

The children explained to everyone how they had forced the black cloud back into the mountain. Then the mountain had shook and the opening in the side blew up. They were sure the spell was destroyed.

The dragon spoke. "You are so brave and I appreciate what you did more than you will ever know. But until we can get the spell book back, the professor will be able to make the potion again and we will continue to fight the fog."

Annie said, "The Leaf Fairy told us what to do. Nate and Gib and I are going to make a forgetting potion and find a way to give it to the professor. Then he will forget the whole thing. She said we must get the book back. The professor stole it so taking it back is not stealing, it is claiming your property. So we need to get the book and give him the potion. We just can't figure out how to do that."

George said, "Well, the professor knows Zoe and Camille, so they can't go back to the museum, at least not until he forgets. Annie, you and the guys need to make the forgetting potion. I guess I'll be the one to steal the book and give him the potion."

Jim spoke up. "I have a better idea. He doesn't know your mom or me. We can go to the museum and tell him that we have also found a dragon and we want to work with him to capture it. I think we need to bring the little kids along since he won't want them to distract us while we talk. We can send them out into the museum to explore the exhibits, but they will really sneak into his lab, find the book, and take it. You can use your fairy powers to fly the book out of the museum.

"Then you can bring the professor a cup of tea to thank him for letting you explore the museum. The potion can be in the tea."

Sara turned and hugged her husband. "Brilliant! You really are a part of the dragon's team. Any questions?"

"Just in case that professor tries something, Zoe and I will stay here to protect the dragon. Camille, you can help, too."

The dragon objected. "Wait a minute. All of you could be in danger with this crazy professor. I should be the one to do all of this. I can't allow the little ones to go into that muscum. And Sara, you and Jim shouldn't have to confront that madman."

Sara put her hand on the dragon's claw. "How many times did you rescue me and my brothers? How often have you taken care of my children and their friends? Mr. Dragon, we know that this spell will take away your magic. Jim and I don't have to worry about that and the professor doesn't know about Annie and Nate's powers. It is far safer for us to do this than you. This one time, let us help you."

The dragon shook his head, but he could see that he was outnumbered since everyone was insisting. "Then I will wait here with Zoe, Camille, and George. But if anything goes wrong, I'll be there in a flash."

"Great! Get the spell ready, Annie."

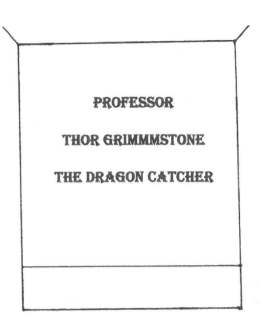

PROFESSOR

THOR GRIMMMSTONE

THE DRAGON CATCHER

Chapter 14

<u>Some Things Must Be Done</u>

Sara, Jim, Nate, and Annie climbed into the minivan. They decided Gib should remain with Camille, Zoe, and George for his own safety. The professor had never seen the minivan since Jim drove his work car to the museum with Zoe and Camille. Jim was sure the professor would not recognize him. Annie carried a small bottle in her pocket. The twins climbed into their car seats and off they went to the museum.

When they arrived at the museum, the four went to the receptionist. "We have some really important information to share with Professor Grimmstone. We need to see him immediately," Jim said.

The receptionist frowned. "The professor is very busy today working in his lab and he told me that he cannot be disturbed. So you will have to come back another day. So sorry." She turned away.

Sara pleaded, "Please, this can't wait. Tell him it has to do with the black fog and what he is trying to catch. Please tell him."

The receptionist stared at them over her spectacles with a questioning look. Then she picked up the phone. "I am so sorry to bother you, Professor...Yes sir, I understand, but.... The woman says she has some information about black fog?... Yes sir, black fog... I'll send them right back."

The receptionist took the four to a door and used her security card to open the door. "You go to the end of the hallway and it is the last door on the left. You can go in, he knows you are coming."

Sara and Jim, Annie and Nate went down the hallway. When they reached the end, Jim pointed to the door on the right. He whispered, "That is where you two need to go when you leave us. Get the book and then bring the tea."

Jim knocked on the door and then they went into the professor's office. He was sitting behind his desk staring at them with his peculiar and scary looking eyes. He spoke cautiously. "So you say you know something about a black fog? That would be an interesting phenomenon."

Sara got right to the point. "Professor Grimmstone, we live near Sugarloaf Mountain and we have been noticing some strange things happening on the mountain. My children keep telling me that they see a dragon flying into a cave at the top of the mountain. I keep telling them that there isn't anything like a dragon. That is just silly.

"But then earlier this afternoon I saw this huge black cloud coming across the sky. I have never seen anything like that. Then I saw these four little people---I could swear they were fairies, but I don't believe in that nonsense either---these four little people were flying across the sky at the fog. I am sure this whole thing sounds crazy. I'm sorry we bothered you, Professor. You must think I am nuts."

"Oh no, no, no. I am very interested. You probably know that I am researching dragons and so I do believe in them. I just haven't found one yet. Why don't we send the little ones out into the museum so we can talk more."

"I guess that would be okay," Jim said. He pointed at the twins. "You two go out and look at all the pretty exhibits. But don't go far and don't go anywhere with anyone else. Do you understand?"

The twins responded together, "Yes, Daddy, we will stay in the museum."

"Such good little children you have. I wish all children could be so obedient. I am sure they would enjoy the dinosaur exhibit. Ask the lady at the front desk to point you in the right direction." The twins left the office and closed the door behind them.

Sara continued, "I have heard that you are researching dragons, so I thought you were the logical person to report this to. It is just so unbelievable to me."

"Yes, yes. Well, some things are just hard to understand and explain. Do you know where this dragon lives exactly?"

Jim went on, "We climbed up the mountain and tried to find his cave since the children were so insistent. I wanted to show them that they were imagining all of this. We couldn't find any cave, but it is pretty rugged up there. He could be hiding anywhere."

"I didn't believe any of this until I saw that black cloud and those little people flying around. And then my children were saying they could see a dragon standing on the top of the mountain, like he was protecting his cave."

"Ah, yes. Let's talk more of this mountain."

*　*　*　*　*　*　*　*

Annie and Nate closed the office door and waited a moment to be sure they weren't followed. Then they crossed the hallway to the lab door and opened it carefully. They went in and closed the door. There were tables full of bottles and bowls and funny looking tubes all over the room. It also smelled pretty bad, kind of like going into their attic at home. The twins had decided to use their telepathy to communicate so no one could hear them. Nate used his fairy power to locate the spell book. He thought really hard about the book and he saw where it was in the lab. Nate moved quickly across the room to a big table.

Nate thought, "Here it is, Annie." Nate tried to lift the book but he could barely get it off the table. "This is a heavy book."

Annie thought to Nate, "We are going to have to use our fairy powers to move it, Nate. There is an open window and the minivan is right over there in the parking lot. Good thing you left the back window open. Let's fly the book over to the van and get out of this lab."

The twins pointed their fingers at the book and it rose into the air. Then they gently pointed across the room and the book flew to the window. They walked to the window and pointed at the van's window. The large spell book floated down and into the car. It was that easy.

Then they found the cafeteria and ordered a cup of green tea. They took the tea to a table and sat down. Annie pulled a bottle of green liquid out of her pocket. "Good thing the Leaf Fairy gave us this forgetting recipe. Let's get this over with." Annie handed the bottle to Nate and he poured the entire contents of the bottle into the teacup. Annie stirred it into the green tea. "Can't even tell we did anything, Annie. Let's go."

The twins carried the cup of tea to the professor's office. He was still seated behind his desk talking to Sara and Jim. "We had fun in the museum. Here professor, we brought you some nice green tea. Hope you like it."

"Such sweet little children. Thank you so much." The professor took the teacup and sipped the tea. He continued to talk with Sara and Jim about dragons. "So you see I have known about this dragon since I was a child. I have collected so much information about him and I finally have him where I can catch him. I will save the world from this evil. And I… Hmmmm….I seem to be forgetting what I was going to say…And why are you two here?"

"Professor, I am sorry that we had to do this. I hope you will forget this encounter as well," Sara said. The professor gently laid his head down on his desk and fell asleep.

Jim and Sara searched the professor's office. They found some folders with information about the dragon and took them. "I think we have found all of his research about our dragon. The rest is so general that he can't connect it to anything. It's time to go."

The family walked out of the museum and climbed into their minivan. "Do you two have the book back there?"

Annie patted the old dusty book as Nate assured his parents that the spell book was safely stowed on the back seat. The family headed home relieved that everything had gone according to the plan. They knew the dragon would be relieved to get his spell book back. And Annie and Nate couldn't wait to tell the Leaf Fairy how well the forgetting spell had worked.

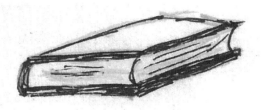

Chapter 15

<u>Did It Work?</u>

Sara, Jim, Nate, and Annie returned home triumphantly displaying the book out the back window. Zoe, George, Camille, Gib, and the dragon cheered. The twins brought the book over to the dragon.

"Here, Mr. Dragon. Your spell book. Better put it in a safe place under lock and key."

"Thank you, children. Sara and Jim, you have been such good people to help me. I cannot say thanks enough times."

Jim spoke for the family, "You have done so much for our family for generations. It is the least we could do to repay you. We expect our relationship to continue for many generations to come."

"It will be my honor to always protect your family." The dragon bowed. "Now I must return this book to its shelf. I will see you all at the clearing tomorrow night for a dragon barbeque. Come hungry!"

"Great! Can't wait. See you then."

The dragon flew to his cave on Sugarloaf Mountain.

Zoe turned to Jim and Sara. "Do we know for sure that this professor will forget everything? Will he stumble across some evidence from his work all these years?"

Sara replied, "Only time will tell, Zoe. We scoured his office for any information he had about our dragon. We figured that his research was a part of the museum's history so we couldn't remove everything. But what he knew about our dragon is right here in these folders and I think the forgetting spell was working quite well when we left. He couldn't even remember why we were in his office and then he fell asleep."

George said, "Perhaps we should pay him a visit tomorrow to see if he remembers Zoe and Camille. Maybe we can see if he still believes dragons exist. Just to be sure."

Camille patted George on the shoulder. "That is a fantastic idea, George! Only I don't think that Zoe and I should approach him directly. He might remember something if he saw our faces."

"So all of you stand nearby pretending to look at an exhibit. I'll ask to speak to the professor since he hasn't seen me before. When he comes out I'll stand in such a way that he can see all of you. I'll ask him some questions about dragons and see what he says."

"Great plan, George," Jim said. "Sara, can you arrange for Camille and Gib to come to the museum with us tomorrow night?"

"I'll take them home now and talk with their mom. I am sure it will be okay."

* * * * * *

George's plan was brilliant. The next day they all went to the museum. Everyone stood nearby looking at an exhibit and George asked the receptionist for the professor. He came out of the door looking right at Zoe and the others. He did not show any recognition of the group. He turned to George. "How may I help you?"

"Thank you so much for seeing me, Professor Grimmstone. I heard that you believe in dragons and I was hoping you could help me find one."

"Young man, that is just silly. Dragons are a part of mythology. I have studied them for many years and I have tried very hard to find any concrete evidence that they exist. But I cannot find anything so I can emphatically tell you that there are no such things as dragons. All pure imagination."

"So you don't think I could trap one?"

"Even if you could find a dragon, if they really exist, their magical powers would overwhelm you. You wouldn't have a chance. So give up that notion. You would do better to learn about archaeology and go dig in the dirt somewhere to find something real from the past. Not these made-up stories."

"Thank you so much for your time, Professor. Have a nice day."

"Thank you for your interest, young man. I plan to write a book about all the dragon mythology and I hope you will read it someday."

They shook hands and George walked out the door. Jim watched the professor and he did not see any recognition of anyone in their group. The professor sounded very convincing and as they left everyone agreed that he had forgotten about their dragon and no longer believed that dragons really existed. That was a great relief to everyone.

They climbed into the minivan and drove home, dropping Camille and Gib at their house. "I hope you two will be able to join us tonight for the barbeque."

"Thanks so much for inviting us, but I think this is one of those times when my parents would really think we were nuts and they probably wouldn't even let us come. We'll catch up with the dragon later. But Zoe, you could bring some of the dragon's ribs to school tomorrow for lunch?"

Zoe laughed. "You bet! I'll make a special plate for you to enjoy. Except we won't tell everyone where the food came from." The girls gave each other a high five and Camille and Gib went into the house. Their parents waved from the front porch.

Chapter 16

The Dragon's Barbeque

It was a beautiful fall evening in late September as the family joined the dragon in the clearing on the mountain for his famous barbeque dinner. Each year the dragon would serve dinner on April first as a welcome to springtime. This was a special occasion and he wanted to celebrate and thank the family for their loyalty and support.

There was a large bonfire in the middle of the clearing and a long picnic table covered with a tablecloth and candles. The dragon had set the table with his finest china and silverware. They could tell he had gone to a lot of trouble to prepare for tonight. They could smell the wonderful odors of the dragon's cooking.

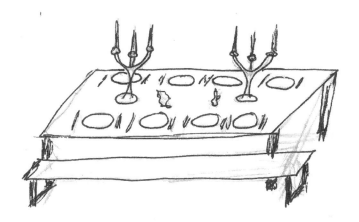

"This dinner is to honor all of your bravery. I hope you will enjoy these famous dragon dishes. I have prepared a wonderful appetizer of bat wings and spider webs mixed with salad greens. Quite a zesty salad dressing as well.

"Then we will have some toad soup made with the finest ingredients. The toads are imported from Brazil and are the tastiest in the world. The broth comes from an old dragon recipe and it is supposed to give you great strength.

"The main course tonight will be my barbeque ribs bathed in the best barbeque sauce in America. There will also be mashed potatoes and green beans.

"For dessert, the Leaf Fairy has graciously made a large honey cake. And I brought some ice cream in a cooler from the local dairy for that final touch. I hope you will enjoy it all."

As they sat down at the table, Annie saw the Leaf Fairy sitting on a small chair in the middle of the table near one of the candlesticks. "Glad you could make it, Leaf Fairy."

"I wouldn't miss one of the dragon's barbeques for anything. The whole Enchanted Forest is jealous that I got to come. I am supposed to talk the dragon into coming to the forest and serving a barbeque dinner there. Do you think he will come?"

"I am sure we can all convince him," Sara said. "It's very nice to meet you, Leaf Fairy. I have heard so much about you."

"And you, Sara, are well known in the forest for the brave deeds that you and your two brothers performed when you visited us long ago."

Jim looked at his four children and whispered, "Is it really safe to eat some of this food? Spider webs and bat wings? And toad soup?"

The children giggled and Nate spoke up. "Dad, we eat this all the time with the dragon and it is delicious. And it will make you big and strong." Everyone burst out laughing because Jim always told the children to eat their dinner so they would be big and strong.

It was a wonderful night. The family enjoyed a scrumptious meal and recalled many of their adventures with the dragon. They sang songs and even danced a bit. By the end of dinner everyone was stuffed and happy as could be.

Except, in the shadows near the clearing, there was someone watching. Professor Grimmstone had been suspicious about George. He wasn't sure if George had really seen a dragon or was just making it up. So he was coming to their house to ask him some more questions when he saw the family climbing the trail to the mountain top. He followed and observed the party.

Since he was an adult, the professor could not see the dragon or the Leaf Fairy, but there was some nagging feeling in his head that he should know what the family was doing having a fancy party in the middle of the woods, even with candles on the table and china. There had to be something that he was missing, that he couldn't remember. He watched closely and heard the people talk several times about a dragon and a fairy, but he never saw them.

The professor returned to the museum that night to check his files. He went through every drawer and searched every shelf. And then he found one folder, only one, that contained a story about a dragon and his family visiting a mall and the king's dragon catcher taking them away to the Black Castle. The father dragon was cast into the Dark Blue Sea while the mother dragon and children were put into prison. This story just seemed too real. Why would he have this article from some mysterious paper if it wasn't true? He would continue to investigate this family and spy on them to learn more. Something was going on here.

*　　*　　*　　*　　*　　*

The dragon thanked the family one last time before they headed down the mountain. The Leaf Fairy helped the dragon clean up the dinner by waving her hand over the table. The dishes were cleaned by the dripping dew from the trees, the fire was extinguished by a simple breath of air, and the tablecloth folded itself neatly into a picnic basket.

In a few moments everything was in order. "Not too hard to do with our magic, Dragon."

"You are right, Leaf. It has been a wonderful evening. I am glad that we were able to defeat the Professor's plan. The children did a magnificent job.

"I wanted to ask for your help, Leaf. You did a terrific job with that forgetting spell. It worked perfectly. Do you know of any remembering spells? To bring back memories?"

"Sometimes it is best to leave things in the past, Dragon. Bringing up old memories is not always a good idea. What is it you want to know?

"The children were reading a book in my library the other day that I thought was just a made-up story. But they were pulled into the book by some magic spell and I had to rescue them. When they came out they said they knew about my family, my wife and children. I couldn't remember ever having a family. But then some memories began to come back. I remembered some things from my past."

"You have a family?"

"The children said that my family was locked away in the Black Castle and then I remembered that I was thrown into the Daek Blue Sea and ended up here. I don't know where this black castle is or how to find it. Can you shed any light on that?"

"Dragon, I do not know about your family. I have never heard of the Black Castle. It is not in the Enchanted Forest. But I do know a very wise owl who may be able to tell you some things. And I will check all of my spell books to see if there is a remembering spell. But you should think carefully if you really want to know of your past. It may be best to leave it alone. Come visit me soon in the forest and we will talk about this again." The Leaf Fairy kissed the dragon on the cheek and then disappeared into the forest as the dragon flew to his cave. He would have to think about finding out about his past.

Suddenly he had a dark feeling in his heart as a professor, miles away, opened a single folder in his office. Something was not right.

And, as they snuggled down into their beds, the four children could feel it, too.

Made in the USA
Charleston, SC
23 December 2016